All Smiles Some Tears Little Fears

Blessing of Stars

Shireen Kalra

Vitasta

Published by
Renu Kaul Verma
Vitasta Publishing Pvt Ltd
2/15, Ansari Road, Daryaganj
New Delhi - 110 002
info@vitastapublishing.com

ISBN: 978-93-86473-77-6

First Edition 2020
MRP ₹ 350

This novel is entirely a work of fiction. Names, characters, events and incidents are entirely imaginary. Reference to real places, actual regions, institutions or community practices has been made in a fictitious manner. Any resemblance to actual persons, living or dead or actual events is purely coincidental.

Typeset & Cover Design by Somesh Kumar Mishra
Printed by Vikas Computer and Printers

Contents

To Dada...

Acknowledgements

With all my love I humbly dedicate my first novel to my grandparents: my dearest dada Shri TR Kalra who will always be the foremost inspiration in my life, my dadi Smt Veena Kalra for introducing me to the world of stories and Indian mythology, my nanu Shri BR Gupta for always going out of his way to support my every endeavour, my nani Smt Sushma Gupta for her endless encouragement and belief in me.

I cannot fully express my gratitude to my wonderful parents, my mom, Mrs Deepti Kalra and my papa, Mr Ranjeet Kalra for always being there for me, every step of the way as I wrote this work.

A big thank you to my biggest fan and toughest critic, my brother, Ruhaan Raj Kalra. You mean the world to me.

A word of appreciation to my friends Ananya Sharma and Mehar Sharma for their affection and faith in this book since day one. A special thanks to my extended family and school friends for their constant support.

I am extremely thankful to my Alma Mater and my respected teachers for nourishing and improving my creative pursuits.

My gratitude to Professor Garima Gupta and her worthy colleagues for their insightful readings of my drafts.

My sincere thanks to my publisher, Ms Renu Kaul Verma and the exceptional team at Vitasta for their dedication and commitment and my editor, Ms Kanagam King for her valuable guidance and hard work.

I would be remiss if I don't thank legendary writers JK Rowling and Ruskin Bond who inspired me to start writing in the first place.

It goes without saying that I am super grateful to all the TV series and romantic comedies I've so dedicatedly watched through my teenage.

And finally, I am really thankful to you, dear reader, for taking out the time to plunge into my imagination. May the *Blessing Of Stars* always be with you.

★★★

The Girl Who dreamt

It was around one am on a snowy winter night. Tucked into the cosy master bed in the Presidential Suite of the Swiss Boutique Hotel, holding a mug of cappuccino in one hand and an evergreen classic in the other; lay Keira Malhotra – an entrepreneur turned business tycoon, who'd been a famous name in the European market for almost two decades now.

Love, fame, power and money all fell into the kitty of this forty-five-year-old Chandigarh girl. With the elegance of royalty, a charming personality and a flair in her commercial game she had secured a satisfactory aggregate of whatever the mundane population longs for.

With a plethora of euphoric memories to cherish and most importantly with stars on her side she had what an onlooker would call the perfect life.

The curtains having fallen on another blessed day of their winter vacation, she put down the novel, reached out to switch off the reading lamp and then dropped her head into the arms of her husband, who lay half-asleep on the other side of the bed. As Keira pulled up the silky quilt, he turned a little, put his arm around her shoulder and gave her an affectionate kiss on the forehead. She thanked God for this moment that couldn't be any better and then with absolutely nothing to worry about, she slowly fell into a sweet–sound sleep, deep into the world of dreams…

It was around one o'clock on a humid summer night. Eighteen-year-old Keira Malhotra – a class 12 commerce stream student – sat upright on the small, congested bed of her Chandigarh room. She sat all alone with nothing for company but a thick file consisting of personal statements, report cards and certificates in one hand and a cup of coffee – she gulped hurriedly to keep awake – in the other. She was gearing up for her *UCAS* application submission. With stress and tension on her mind, she burned the midnight oil while everyone else in the house lay fast asleep.

'THIS' is what the forty-five-year-old Keira dreamed of as a nostalgia enriched sleep flooded her subconscious. Yes, she was dreaming of her 'past', a past that made her what she was today. Maybe this worthwhile day of her vacation spent indulging in spas and chocolates somehow reminded her of her youthful self and all the situations and struggles she had been through to attain the comforts of her present life. Essentially the eighteen-year-old Keira was the very same person but today, the bed was different, the surroundings were changed, the state of affairs had evolved, mostly for the better.

Back in her dream, she saw her young self being overwhelmed when she received the reward for her dedication in the form of an email. It stated that she had been accepted into the prestigious University of Oxford in England and had been offered a place to pursue an undergraduate degree in Economics & Management, along with a fully sponsored scholarship from its Royal Academy.

From the next instant, her dream takes the form of a Disney motion picture with flashes of varied moments projected in front of her closed eyes.

After confronting the expected arguments at home, she buries their unfounded aversion. Taking a fresh step closer to her anticipated life, she bids goodbye to her immediate family at the Indira Gandhi International Airport and walks away towards what she hopes will be the best of the days, hiding her tears as she turns away from loved ones. The next moment she is boarding the 216 British Airways flight to London.

Flying high in the starlit sky that evening, she sees herself parting from all that was familiar, her country, her family and her childhood. This loss of all things familiar was going to transport her from life's first phase to the next one – an independent college life. The child had to grow up now to get ready to face the world, experience all that it had to offer and make decisions, which would later make her and set her free to live her dream.

Golden memories of her childhood came flooding back. She was a fun-loving but studious child. Each memory – playing on her favourite swing that seemed to touch the sky, bicycling along bumpy roads, feeding stray dogs, making mud toys, playing cricket with the boys or climbing up the mango tree, spending vacations at her maternal grandparents' house, fighting with cousins over the TV remote, late night drives and café gossips, sharing tiffin with friends in class – felt so fresh and yet so distant now.

Her mind sank deep into thought. She recalled her motives for making this decision, the reason for going off so far away. She reminded herself of all the people she had defied. She cautioned herself against losing her goals amidst the innumerable attractions the big city had to offer that could lead you astray – drinks and drugs, clubs and shops and the playboys.

As the plane flew over the Gothic city of London, from her window seat she looked down mesmerized and thrilled to actually witness all the phenomenal grandeurs till now seen only in movies. Right below her awestruck eyes was the London eye, the Buckingham Palace, the Westminster's Palace along with the gigantic Big Ben and the revolutionary Tower Bridge across the sparkling blue Thames River. Everything shone bright in the orange light of the setting sun that evening and everything to her seemed so bejewelled and magnificent.

Life unveiled a brand new chapter as Keira finally came out of the Heathrow Airport pushing her luggage trolley. She could sense that her dreams had already started to come true as she walked on ready to live, laugh and love…

★★★

To New Beginnings

Keira moved towards the first double decker that would take her to Oxford. But as she climbed up its steps – camera in hand – ready to capture her first moments in college – her foot stumbled and the camera slipped out of her hand. Reflexively she closed her eyes; her heart skipped a beat at the thought of her camera hitting the floor. But it didn't. The quick acting hands of a tall and handsome Indian boy, who was just behind her, had saved it.

He said nothing as he handed over the camera and moved on towards the upper deck of the bus. Keira looked at him for a second and then followed, finding her seat along the way.

Night had fallen. The classy streetlights came up as the bus started its journey from London to Oxford. With the night wanderers roaming in the parks and the party animals queuing up in front of the clubs, the atmosphere was typically English – a mingle of modern times and ancient culture that she had always admired.

Within an hour and a half the bus dropped her off at the Central Entrance of the University from where she made her way to the impressive Christ Church College office. As the main college building of the place that had always seemed like a second *Hogwarts* to her came into sight for the very first time her heartbeat got faster.

'Welcome to the University of Oxford,' greeted a friendly male face at the admissions desk, who checked her letter, completed a few formalities and then handed over the responsibility to Miss Smith, her Resident Assistant who would escort her to her hostel room and acquaint her with other necessary details.

'You're going to love it here,' she warmly smiled at Keira who was enthralled by the Hall of Fame behind.

Her eyes followed the portrait frames of distinguished Oxford alumni: Stephen Hawking, Albert Einstein, Hugh Grant, Bill Clinton, the Royals, Imran Khan, Emma Watson and Indira Gandhi among other prominent faces that hung there proudly. She felt a sudden yearning to bag a place for herself up there in the coming years. She then followed her Resident Assistant.

'Oxford is very caring towards it's Undergrads,' was the first thought that struck her mind as she entered her – soon to be home – room; room number six on the first floor. Her roommate was an Indian Mumbai girl who introduced herself as Sasha.

Keira called her father and gave him an update. The two roommates sharing the same motherland found each other reassuring in this foreign land and spent the next hour getting to know each other. They had dinner and chatted about various things ranging from common topics like selection of subjects to future goals and past endeavours.

The next morning the August sunlight entered through the windowpane, cut through the curtains, crawled onto the bed and then caressed a sleeping Keira's eyes. God's rays of hope had found their way to her from above the clouds in the form of sunlight that lit her face. Waking up she went straight towards the window, drew the curtains and took in her first morning at Oxford.

In front of her was a grey marbled walking path. Dew-laden lush green grass grew along its sides. Right next to it was the endless lake where punting took place. Across the lake was a wooden over bridge that led further into the university. The beauty of it all was enhanced by two mighty oak trees opposite the hostel entry. Brown metal benches were scattered between them. It seemed like the perfect place to de-stress or even to complete assignments.

With a smile on her radiant face, she quickly freshened up, got dressed, slipped on a light overcoat and a cotton scarf and headed towards the Christ Church dining hall with an equally excited Sasha. As they walked enjoying the pleasant weather, amidst students – some carrying bags, some on their bicycles – she came across the famous main meadow of Christ Church Cathedral with a circular fountain in the middle from where emerged paths, each leading to a different part of the college. The buildings around embellished in a dusky brown shade…600 years of architectural history… the ways of the old harmonising beautifully with the new. Yes! She was finally here, at Oxford.

A special welcome breakfast had been organized on account of the term beginning at the Great Hall, a hall that indeed stood up to its name. Students were already settling on the long wooden tables interacting with ease, as if they had known each other since high school. Soon the faculty members arrived on the raised platform in the front. As Keira and Sasha took their places, Professor Dippet, the managing director of faculty stood up to address the students, specially the freshmen.

'Welcome dear students to another great year at Oxford and a warmer welcome to all the bright new faces that join us for the first time today,' he said. 'We here at Christ Church will make sure to groom you into fully skilled and knowledgeable individuals who are masters in their chosen fields...'

Keira was listening attentively, when the sound of doors opening distracted her and many others. Four besuited students, led by the same boy Keira had seen the previous night, entered together and walked straight to the empty space in front of the platform with a disgusting air of superiority and swag.

Professor Dippet chose to ignore them and went on instructing, 'Your introductory orientation will begin in two hours and you are requested to contact Mr Brown after finalising your classes; a final reminder that the Cathedral is forbidden to all except on Fridays.' And then in a loud and clear voice he declared, 'Let the feast, begin,' and out came a number of waiters carrying mouth-watering dishes that were served efficiently on each table even as the first years stared at them or the amazing paintings that hung around.

Keira and Sasha had just begun with forks and knives in their hands, when a native guy sitting opposite them introduced himself, 'Hey, I'm Steve.'

'Hey Steve,' Sasha replied enthusiastically, 'I'm

Sasha.' Keira introduced herself too as Sasha went on, 'you do have a cute British accent...'

'Yup...My home is not far, and you guys are from... India?'

And just like that they became acquaintances and headed together for the orientation.

Interacting with other ambitious and like-minded students, walking in strange hallways, coping with a totally different lifestyle and food, Keira felt a little intimidated on the first day. However, she could not let it get to her. Oxford was the perfect place for the kind of person she was and aspired to become: elegant, cultured, broad minded and progressive, all at the same time. In order to be selected she had done everything humanly possible from maintaining straight A's, performing volunteer work, taking up internships, publishing works and serving in the school student council. Securing a place among the finest minds of the world here at Oxford had added brilliance to this list of her achievements.

She spent the weekend before term commenced getting ahead in her reading lists and devoted Sunday to her wanderlust. She took a ride to London and spent the day breezing through the city in a double decker bus, walking through the west ends, listening to the chimes of the Big Ben, ogling the jewels at the Tower…basically doing all that was possible during that short visit for this was London – Europe at its best. A city with an impressive slate of sights, entertainment and eateries, a city perpetually at your service offering a chance to witness the microcosm of the once mighty British empire. A day so small – even a year – was not enough to explore every nook and corner or to get a peep into the deepest tales the city had to tell.

The bus stopped at the terminal station. She walked across the London Bridge, a massive reminder of London's expansion during the industrial revolution; to start her journey from the place London did – the 950-year-old Tower of London. With her headphones on and a warm noon sun making her hair sparkle in the breeze, she strolled through London's political centre, both historic and contemporary.

Of the many gifts London has given to the world, none has been greater than that of literature and if there is a city that reads like an epic saga, it is London. There standing on the Westminster Bridge she was reminded of the words of William Wordsworth who on a similar morning of 1802 stood there, where today after two centuries, Keira and so many others paused to witness the very same mesmerizing splendour the city continued to offer:

silent bare Ships, towers, theatres, domes and chapels lie,
Open into the fields and to the sky,
all bright and glittering in smokeless air.

She resumed her walk and moved towards the Westminster Palace, a building of sandstone from where London is now ruled. Then she passed by the Boadicea, and moved down to the lively parliament square, across the jam-packed Whitehall where the officials resided. Then came the Cenotaph built as a tribute to the victims of the two futile world wars; followed by the famous 10 Downing Street and a passing glance at the Buckingham Palace and gardens. She halted at a café in the thriving centre of London – the Trafalgar Square, which with all its statues, fountains and people felt somewhat familiar.

She bought a frappe and took a foot expedition through the Convent Garden, crossing a few streets, asking directions from strangers to reach the largest of the royal parks of Kensington Palace – the Hyde Park where its pre-dusk wanderers had already begun to appear.

There as she sat on one of the wooden benches admiring the lake, she saw an elderly couple sitting hand in hand on the opposite side. They seemed to be genuinely happy, not concerned about people who walked by or like Keira observed them from a distance; they just sat there completing one another, which made

Keira wonder if she too would ever be able to court such a fortunate fate.

It was almost five o'clock. The sun had started to set. Keira took a taxi back to Central London to the millennial London Eye. Having already booked her place earlier, she jumped the crowd to enter one of the capsules that went up into the sky to become one with the overwhelming skyline of the Metropolitan, with the Shard and the Gherkin standing out as the tallest.

As she saw a flock of birds flying by, she felt like a bird flying about in an alien city, far away from the old flock; the only exception being that she was not the bird that got left behind, she was the bird that flew away the farthest.

After a fulfilling day of random explorations, she gave a final salute to the Thames River until their next meet and walked down one of the empty streets whose end she couldn't see; with a backpack on and a youthful song she went where the road took her.

★★★

Little Big Influences

It is perhaps only when away from home, facing joys and tears all on your own that one actually discovers who one really is; that is when the true self comes out. While some welcome it gracefully, others continue with attempts to push it back into its previous shell assuming it is safe there, away from influences. However, the truth is that with this newly found dilemma of who one is, comes a threat of being influenced; every memory, every experience is capable of influencing one. For the better or the worse only time would tell.

As the fresher week unfolded in the University of Oxford, both the city and its new occupants began showing and discovering their true colours. With the Michaelmas Term in full swing, challenging course sessions and friendly interactions with newfound acquaintances in the junior common room, Keira had come to appreciate this new life.

Sasha had developed a crush, just like many others on a flamboyant senior, Carter and attempted to earn a rank among the 'Queen Bees'. Steve had joined the college sports club and had cracked the trial to the varsity football team. As for Keira, she had made quite an impression on everyone from the tutors who liked her prospects to the boys who gave her attention for her pretty face to the sorority who gave her attention to know the reason behind the attention of the boys.

As the term passed by Sasha, Steve and Keira became good friends, sitting together during lectures and lunch and hanging out in cafes, libraries and parks afterwards.

One late evening when Keira came into her room, she found Sasha dressed up in a sparkling little dress, applying heavy mascara.

'Going somewhere?' she enquired.

'Oh yeah, Allison and Holly are taking me to the opening of this new night club in east Oxford, a small girls night out you know,' she winked, 'You know, you should come too. Maybe I can ask them for an extra pass.'

'Me, nah…, she refused. 'Too damn tired,' she

lied, as Sasha went out leaving Keira lying on her bed, wide-awake.

It had merely been half a term and Keira did not want to indulge in the party routines and other such stuff, that she felt would distract her from her goal even as she tried to cope with her personal shortcomings and properly adapt to the much-changed surroundings.

Sasha returned around three in the morning, waking Keira with a loud knock. Keira turned on the lights and opened the door to find Sasha completely drunk with her heels in her hands and her eyes smudged.

'Did everything go well?' she asked, even though Sasha's gestures indicated otherwise.

'Nooo,' she exclaimed partially leaning on the wall, while Keira made an effort to guide her to the bed, 'You know who was there? Huh?'

'Who?'

'Carter,' she said, the name followed by a sob.

'So…?'

'So, I went up to him and asked him for a dance.'

'And…Did he say yes?'

'Of course not,' she gave a laugh as she tumbled on her bed. He said, 'I am sorry, but I'm not interested,' she mimicked as Keira went to turn off the light, 'Keira, he rejected me, I got rejected.'

Now was it Sasha speaking or the alcohol? It was hard to tell.

'You know Keira, my best friend from high school...,' she recalled, 'She had the perfect boyfriend. They looked super adorable together. God I was so jealous! Not that I couldn't find one myself. I mean there were a few, but nothing that interested me for more than a summer.'

'Don't worry Sasha, you'll find yourself an amazing boy and you guys will be the most adorable couple on campus,' Keira assured.

'You really think so?'

'Yes!'

'Awwwee...come give me a hug.' Sasha wrapped her arms tightly around Keira, nearly choking her.

'You know what? There is this other hottie, the one who bosses his way around. He's tall and rugged...,' she drooled, 'I think you'd like him. Should I set you up?'

'Sasha!'

'Oh wait, I can't even set myself up, how will I set you up!'

'Doesn't matter, coz I don't want to be set up,' she replied, 'Now sleep.' She tucked her into bed.

That night Keira's thoughts kept her from falling asleep. Would Sasha really find the perfect guy? Does a 'perfect guy' actually exist? Rubbish. All she knew was that Sasha must be told to amend her regular clubbing habits.

'Not again! Oh God Keira, sleep,' said an annoyed Sasha as Keira sat on the table preparing notes for the semester exams which were a week away.

The term was about to end and with a bunch of pending essays and a fast approaching deadline, managing all the work was becoming harder than it seemed.

'Ok, ok, I will.' Keira switched off the lamp for five minutes until Sasha fell asleep and then again switched it on. This practice continued until the final paper had been handed over for assessment.

The continuous row of papers got over within a blink of the eye and soon it was time for the results. Though these particular ones didn't really make a difference to the final degree, yet these were the very first of the evaluations and would reflect where each of the brilliant students stood in class; it was an opportunity to prove your wit and ability and analyse your potential.

The morning of the result, the dining hall and *JCR* (Junior Common Room) were empty, as all the students had gathered near the notice board, where the results were displayed. Sasha and Keira sat in one corner of the corridor anxiously waiting when Steve returned with a satisfied look.

'What is it?' Sasha inquired, as they both stood up.

'Well, you and I are somewhere in the middle,' he paused as Sasha smiled, 'and you Keira are the one with the top grade.' 'Whoa Keira, you stood first!' She jumped to hug Keira who was still trying to soak in the good news, 'This calls for a celebration. C'mon Keira; you cannot refuse! Tonight the drinks are on you.'

That night the three got all dressed up for a celebration and agreed to go to a city pub of Sasha's choice where as expected the queue was way too long. With the term ending and the results out most of the first years had decided to celebrate in the same way and so they all waited and waited in the never-ending entry line.

It was around 11 pm. Just as the trio was about to reach the entry point the very flashy gang, with the boy Sasha had spoken about to Keira earlier leading the way, walked towards the pub entrance with their usual air of superiority.

The boy patted the bouncers shoulder as they opened the doors for the group. He gave a slight smirk and was the first to walk in, followed by the other three including a girl who much to Sasha's surprise winked at Steve, who just like all other people tired after hours of waiting in the queue stood gaping at the group.

After a few more minutes of waiting the doors were finally opened for the trio and they stepped into an area with florescent lights, blaring bass that made the room quake, dancing bodies tangled together, a high ceiling with awesome lights hanging from it, a long lit-up bar, and a balcony upstairs with booths to sit and chill.

Keira tried to adjust her eyes to the darkness and the blinking disco lights; loud music reverberated through her body making her feel a bit out of place. Sasha already feeling at home introduced her to a few guys she had never seen before. The colourful night – full of tequila shots, R&B electric beats and dancing – was marred by the sound of breaking glass followed by a groan.

Apparently the arrogant boy who they had seen earlier had smashed an entire bottle of vodka right into the head of another who fell on the bar table. The guy was rescued by his friends, who made a strong attempt to get back at that Indian boy, starting a scuffle between both the groups. The situation got under control only when seeing the events taking a nasty violent turn the club security was summoned and all of them were thrown out.

'I wonder why these people spoil the reputation of the college,' remarked Steve as they walked through the exit a few minutes later. With the music now low, they could finally hear each other and began to discuss what was to become the hot gossip topic of the week.

'Moreover he is from India, what kind of impression will he leave of our country?' Sasha complained as Keira nodded in agreement.

'You guys hold on for a minute. I have to use the restroom,' Keira said and walked away giving Sasha a chance to question Steve about the *winking beauty.*

It was when Keira came out of the loo that she again encountered the boy. This time he was standing adjacent to the wall of the men's restroom, trying to calm down a frail looking boy.

'Buddy, it's ok, you are going to be fine,' he said convincingly, holding the boy's shoulders. 'I promise you Lucas will never mess with you again,' he assured him; following it with an aggressive pat on the back and a brotherly hug.

It was only after they stepped apart that Keira noticed blood on the frail boy's shirt, blood that dripped onto the floor from the aggressive boy's hands, but he didn't seem to care.

'What are you looking at?' demanded the *winking beauty* who appeared from behind. Keira without responding started walking towards Sasha who had just had a heated discussion with Steve about the girl, but he remained secretive.

As they walked towards the main road of the Oxford city, they saw a Limo halt right in front of the boy. He could hardly stand straight and was clenching his bleeding hand, of which he now seemed to be aware. Within a matter of seconds, the chauffeur got out and went on to open the rear door. However, the boy gestured him to stop; he then went on to open the door by himself with visible effort; his face twisting in pain as he attempted to close the door once he sat. Keira observed him keenly while Sasha and Steve continued to quarrel. There was something remarkably strange in his demeanour, which she found worth knowing.

They had only a fortnight more to spend in the frozen winter land of Oxford. Everyone was busy packing, returning lent books, collecting evaluated essays and buying keepsakes for friends and family. Keira having completed the formality of buying presents, which anyways would be despised, sat quietly in the Bodleian Library pursuing additional reading material for future essays.

Steve arrived at her table just as Keira was finishing the second last chapter of Fisher's *Elementary Problems of Economics*. He was looking a little worried.

'Keira, Sasha has got another invite to a sorority club party. This time it is outside the city,' he said expressing concern, as Keira closed the book to pay attention.

'Again!' She exclaimed. 'That too on a week day; what is wrong with her?'

'Keira, I think something is wrong with her. She has been acting all freaked out since the day the session ending was announced. She hasn't been eating. I see her in the market roaming near those creepy gift shops. She ignores me,' he said. Seeing Keira's knitted brows he continued, 'and looking at your expression it seems she hasn't talked about it to you either.'

'I guess it has something to do with her family. I mean in my case I am the one who calls home every time, but her parents – they call every day.'

'So? I go home every weekend, mine don't call at all.'

'I think she's worried she won't be able to stand up to their expectations. She once mentioned that her family is so over the top that it won't surprise her if the whole society was waiting for her arrival at the gate.'

'You think it is this pressure that is troubling her?'

'It is possible. But who doesn't face pressure?' she sighed, 'Look at me, my parents; they don't expect anything from me, like anything at all. I face a different kind of pressure – pressure to prove them wrong. And if you haven't noticed I have been cherishing dinner conversations that don't involve criticism. I myself am not that eager to go home. But does that mean that I indulge in alcohol all through the night, every night, to distract myself from the reality check I'm about to get once holidays are declared in this fantasy land?'

'So should we talk to her?' he asked.

'Talk to whom?' popped Sasha who'd just arrived

panting, 'I have been looking for you everywhere in the campus. There is this amazing party tonight and I wanted to check if you guys are interested. Hurry up and decide. They are going to run out of passes,' she announced as Steve and Keira exchanged a deciding look and asked her to sit.

'Sasha don't get offended, we are your friends…' Steve began.

'I very well know that, and that is why I am taking you to the most amazing party,' she said eagerly.

'Sasha you say that about every party,' complained Keira. 'You have to stop this. I am tired of opening the door every night at 3 am.'

'If that's the case I can stay over at Allison's after the party.'

'That's not the point,' interrupted Steve. 'What we mean to say is that this habit of yours, of clubbing every night, it isn't good. We ourselves would support it once in a while, just not every second day,' he tried to explain.

'Oh c'mon you two; don't be such bores,' she said. 'If not now, when?'

'Sasha there's a limit to everything,' asserted Steve.

'Why don't you go and tell this to that *winking girl* of yours, Veronica isn't it?' She sounded jealous. 'You know what, you guys are just jealous that I get all these invites while you spend your evenings with your laptop. Steve you fear that I'll turn out to be better friends with them,' she flared up 'and Keira why don't you for once accept you want to be in that league?' She rose up and stormed out of the library.

'Do you think I said something that hurt her?' inquired Steve.

'No, don't worry she'll come around,' Keira reassured him, though she herself wasn't sure.

★★★

The Cherished Stroll

The New Year brought many changes for Keira in the University. The beginning of the Hilary Term in January brought with it the much-awaited announcement of the student's union election. Keira though not entirely sure of her chances, on constant pestering from both Steve and Sasha got her name entered against Lucas for the post of vice president; little did she know that the very day of registration would end in such a mess that she would doubt her decision immediately.

After a long day of strained election discussions, mixed responses and tedious research for yet another complex essay, Keira slowly walked out of the Bodleian

Library with a pile of books in her hand and an exhausted mind when suddenly out of nowhere appeared in her way Lucas and his loyal acquaintances turned supporters for the forthcoming elections.

'Hey everyone, look who is here,' ridiculed Andy, one of Lucas' girlfriends calling out to the bunch of students who sat around her and Lucas, who looked exactly like one of those rich spoilt brats, infamous and dominating.

'Who?' a few of them asked teasingly.

'Well, a silly little girl who daydreams that she can defeat my Lucas, our Lucas,' barked Andy proudly as she got up and ambled towards Keira. 'So anything more interesting or perhaps realistic you fantasize about in broad daylight. Huh, honey?'

'Or maybe some fantasies stored for times when there's no light,' added another guy flirtatiously. Lucas himself joined in the lionizing and got up, followed by all the others who rose up too as if to show respect for the pack leader.

'C'mon love we are eager to hear you out; you must have something to share that'll redeem our poor souls,' he mocked.

'I do, plans that would never fit in your head,' protested the inner voice which at that precise moment failed to find its way out of her choked mouth as she stood dumbstruck by the sudden attack.

'Hurry up honey, do you think we have the whole day,' Andy took a rowdy step and pushed Keira's bosom with a force making her drop her books in reflex.

'No we don't,' continued Lucas as he also moved closer to her but before he could even think of harming her a muscular hand came from behind and grabbed Lucas' shoulder, eliciting raged reactions from the pack members.

'Back off you bastard, roared the very same Indian guy who was fighting him the other night in the club, as Lucas turned around to face him. One of Lucas' braver friends tried to free him and got punched with such force that he almost collapsed.

Holding Lucas by his unbuttoned collar he acridly warned, 'Stay away from her if you want to **stand** in the election.' He stared into his eyes, which were equally enraged to see him. 'Now all of you move!' he commanded.

Lucas murmured as they left, 'only for the election's sake…otherwise...'

'You all right?' the boy asked Keira who simply stood there bewildered with tears in her eyes. He picked up the books and handed them over.

She breathed a faint *thank you* and walked away without another word for she had nothing left to say. The incident had left her feeling weak and humiliated that a boy, a boy had to come and defend her – save her; that she wasn't strong enough to save herself. Though she was thankful to the stranger, she felt ashamed that she hadn't been able to do anything. To her it didn't feel like the others had underestimated her but rather that she had overestimated herself.

The next day Keira Malhotra seemed to walk around with much more confidence than usual. It is true what they say – we always pretend to be something we are not, to own something we actually don't have and thus, maybe on that snowy day when Keira lost her self-confidence she made an effort to pretend as if she owned the darn thing. She did not talk to anyone about it, as she felt it would only complicate things more. She had however made up her mind that if she encountered any one or even all of them now she would take them on single-handedly.

The day passed with mixed proportions of cold and election gossip flowing through the air. In the evening when Sasha and Keira were returning to the hostel, an oddly recognizable voice called out from behind.

'Hey,' the saviour of the previous day said as he reached the two girls.

'Hi...' Sasha drooled. He responded with a nod while Keira looked at him in dilemma.

'I was just thinking if maybe you'd like to talk,' he asked.

Yes, after last night, Keira did feel the need to talk to someone…maybe him, the only other person apart from her foes who'd witnessed her momentary helplessness.

'Ok…sure.'

Signalling Sasha that she would see her later at the hostel she went with him thinking of suitable words to start a conversation. She didn't really have a good impression of this charming guy standing next to her but coming to think of it, things had started to change a little.

'I'm Cabir, Cabir Dhawan. Second year English Literature,' he said extending his hand. Keira shook it. It was warm and strong.

'Keira Malhotra,' she replied. 'Fresher, Economics Management.'

'Well, I've seen you around a couple of times, and after yesterday's incident, I felt maybe it would be good if we got to know each other,' he said. 'Now that we have a common enem…' he started to say but was interrupted by Keira.

'Thank you for last night, I am really very grateful,' she said relieved to be able to express her gratitude which she had been unable to do the previous day. She had felt guilty about it. 'I'm sorry for just walking away. I wasn't quite right in my mind.'

'Oh, that was nothing. They are just a bunch of jerks, scared of fighting back,' he assured her as they now strolled in the streets of Central Oxford.

'Just don't take them seriously,' he added 'and yeah don't worry; they won't come anywhere near you. Now that we hate the same person, I'll make sure I teach them any lessons required or perhaps pending,' he smirked. Keira noticed her heart skip a beat.

'I don't like hate, hate him,' she said.

'I do,' he said firmly. Anger and hate reflected clearly in his eyes.

'Why, what's he done to you?' she asked, 'Did he bully you?'

Cabir responded with a mysterious sarcastic laugh leaving Keira puzzled.

'What happened yesterday though?' he asked deftly changing the direction of the conversation.

'Nothing extreme thanks to you; they were roasting me because I'm standing against Lucas in the elections... but now I'm having second thoughts. I might just withdraw,' she paused.

'And that is exactly what they want – you backing out,' he said as though completely attuned to their intentions. 'You won't do that and let them win, now will you?'

Keira kept quiet, so he continued, 'you will win, especially if the person standing against you is that jerk; mark my words.'

Keira's face lit up a bit as he spoke.

'In fact you don't seem to be one of those girls who need to be rescued, you make the other lot.'

'What?'

'The way you conduct yourself...you are one of those who don't need protection, you're among those who boys need protection from,' he said with a smile. Keira laughed. He continued, 'I'm certain even if I hadn't been there you would have kicked some ass yourself. It's just that seeing you there I had to come.'

'Maybe you are right,' she nodded and fell silent as words failed her.

Had Cabir read her mind or was he just saying things to comfort her? She didn't know. All she knew was that someone else was just speaking out aloud what she had been telling herself all day.

'You want to go grab some coffee?' he asked confidently as they strolled past a popular café.

'Coffee sounds good,' she agreed.

'You know I too have seen you around,' she said changing the topic. 'I don't know if you remember; the day I boarded my first bus to Oxford, you saved my precious camera from tumbling down into the pavement. Thanks for that too.'

They exchanged smiles as they now sat on one of the café tables waiting for their order. 'And then one day at the club, where you were beating Lucas yet again,' she continued , 'I've heard that you are quite a bully, you don't seem like one though.'

'I'll take that as a compliment, if you will,' he said plainly. 'So Keira Malhotra, how's your trajectory been so far,' he politely asked, while taking a sip of his freshly brewed cappuccino.

'Okay…' she smiled amused by the unusual question. 'I'm from Chandigarh, nineteen-years-old, police background, here on scholarship, studying Business… Hoping to becoming an entrepreneur,' she said. 'And… that is it,' she paused seeing the smile on his face.

'Economics…huh? So your maths must be real good?'

'Maybe,' she said modestly.

'I really sucked at it…Thank God it's over!' Keira couldn't help laughing at his funny expression.

'Enough about me,' she said. 'Everyone likes talking about themselves; that's how you engage people, and if something common comes out, even better…so tell me about yourself.'

'Well,' he said adopting the same pattern of introduction, 'In that case I am from Delhi, living in London, business background, twenty-years-old, lived in boarding schools, not here on scholarship.' He paused, took a sip of his coffee and continued, 'I'm a philosopher, a bibliophile, a travelholic and like you mentioned earlier a delinquent spoilt brat.' Keira smiled at the extensive use of writer's vocabulary.

'Ma'am, are you done?' asked the waiter

'Yes,' said Keira. Cabir nodded as they put down their mugs and rose.

'Would you please get me the bill?' Keira asked

'It has already been cleared, Mr Dhawan is a regular customer,' he said and handed over a brownie box to Cabir before walking away.

'But…Cabir, there is no need for it,' she said surprised when he gave her the walnut brownie. 'Thank you, I had a great time,' she said honestly, as they walked out of the cafe.

Keira was to head back to her dorm but Cabir insisted of walking with her. After a short walk to the entrance of her hostel Cabir bid goodbye.

'I appreciate you having spared me some time,' he smiled. Keira noticed how adorably his eyes lit up and two dimples resembling a naughty child appeared on his cheeks when he did.

'Since we're in the same college I hope that I get to see you soon,' she said hopefully.

'I will find you, soon enough,' he assured her and turned to leave. Keira walked towards the door, waving him a final good bye when her eyes fell on Sasha, standing on the balcony of their room.

Probably having seen them walking together, she waved eagerly at Keira. Keira headed up ready to answer the missile of questions she knew Sasha would fling at her.

'So how was your sweet little romantic stroll?' Sasha began straightaway as Keira entered the room.

'It was nothing of that sort…' she said putting the brownie on the table.

'Keira, don't be so uninteresting…just look at him!' she swooned.

'So? I hardly know him.'

'Pretty soon you will know those eyes and that smile that can melt an iceberg.'

'When did you check him out so carefully?'

'I'm Sasha, Keira, do you even have to ask me this?' she winked as she went on to pick up the brownie, while Keira, turned to the other side of the room to hang her overcoat. 'So did he give it to you,' she asked in a teasing tone.

'No, what makes you think he would?' She denied at once but couldn't conceal the blush spreading on her face.

'So then you bought it for us?'

'Bought what?' she asked turning around only to find the brownie in her hand. Her face turned red when she realized she had misunderstood Sasha.

'Oh, you thought about something else, didn't you?' Sasha teased. 'You can tell me you know,' she taunted.

'I thought nothing and yes the brownie is a gift from him, Cabir.' She breathed a sigh of relief and grabbing her nightwear rushed into the washroom as Sasha continued to laugh.

The next few days there was no sight of Cabir and in spite of Sasha's repeated attempts Keira too showed no interest in finding him either, until one afternoon she saw him and his friends walking past the corridor of Christ Church.

'Hey,' she greeted Cabir, who stopped and greeted her back while his friends exchanged surprised looks.

'How's life?' he asked looking charming as ever.

'Spectacular.'

'People, this is Keira,' he turned to his friends who appeared rather taken aback, 'and Keira these are my people – Kris, Veronica, Nate and Sid.' He introduced them one by one; none of them bothered to shake her hand; they just gave feeble lopsided smiles.

'So you are the one standing against Lucas?' Sid asked, casting an assessing look.

'Ah...yeah,' she confirmed smiling at Cabir who smiled back as their eyes made contact. They were interrupted by a hissing voice that called out to her from behind a pillar.

'Keira!' It was Steve, who for some reason seemed to be hiding behind a pillar. 'Come here please, it is urgent,' he pleaded.

'Excuse me for a bit, I'll be back,' she told them and rushed towards the pillar immediately.

'Steve, is everything ok? Why are you hiding?' she asked nearing him.

'What are you doing? Why are you even talking to those people? he asked instead of answering her. 'Trust me, you don't want to be seen with this lot specially not when the elections are nearing!'

'But why, what's wrong?' she argued.

'I'll explain later, come along Sasha is waiting,' he said, pulling her by the arm. She tried looking back only to find that Cabir and his friends had already gone. Perhaps they too were not that eager to continue the conversation.

'Steve, please just let it out. What is wrong?' Keira begged as they now sat in the JCR with Sasha.

'I can't. All right! It will only get you in trouble.'

'I mean what could possibly be that wrong, after all he was nice to me,' she wondered aloud.

'And hot too,' added Sasha.

'Steve I need to know,' Keira insisted.

'Ok fine. But you cannot repeat what I tell you now. You take it to your grave or Cabir will dig one for you.'

They both promised never to talk about it. Steve took an audible breath and said, 'Cabir Dhawan – he's the reason I'm out of the football team.'

'When did this happen!' exclaimed Sasha.

'And why on earth did you not tell us?'

"That's what I'm trying to tell you now,' he said. 'It happened when the term began, I was at the cheerleader trials, and I tried flirting with the head cheerleader and she happened to be Veronica, Cabir's friend.'

'So?'

'So I became their next target.'

'What target?'

'It's like entering their "to torture" hit list. They make certain that it counts among your life's worst memories.'

'And what is this hit list?'

'Keira, do you even know these people?'

'No I don't, I just met them and thanks to you the conversation didn't even last half a minute,' she complained.

'Do you Sasha?'

'Not really.'

'Dear God! What amazing friends I've have, totally

unaware of what is happening around them,' he looked heavenwards, 'one busy with her books and the other parties.'

'Not anymore,' corrected Sasha, who had been trying to curb her habit.

'Cabir and his gang are like one big family, they always stick together. You mess with one; you have to face all of them. They are self-absorbed egoistic bastards…,' he said angrily. 'You don't want to mess with them. They'll go to any extent in the name of friendship,' he warned. 'If anyone tries saving their target they become the next victim. They often get suspended by the authorities, but man they don't care,' he said pausing to catch a breath.

'You said you were their target, so what did they do?'

'Cabir is the captain of the varsity football team,' stated Steve.

'Whoa...' began Sasha but she quickly shut up when Steve glared at her.

'So he got one of his contacts to put red ants into my shoes during the trials,' he said, 'At first I didn't suspect a thing, but once I began to play, I felt this terrible stinging sensation; I couldn't concentrate. The ants climbed up my shorts and the itching became unbearable; I had to leave the field.'

'That was awfully devious,' agreed Sasha.

'I reacted badly to the bite and could not attend the

rest of the trials. So the coach dropped me,' he said angrily, his eyes reflecting the loathing he felt for the gang.

'And that's why you didn't show up for classes; there was no family gathering, was there?' Keira concluded.

'Yes, and that is why I am warning you Keira, not bargaining or arguing but telling you – stay away from them or you will land up in trouble.'

'But don't you think I should talk to Cabir. Don't ask me why but I think he might listen,' she suggested.

She had not mentioned their little coffee chat to Steve and after listening to him, she didn't dare to.

'Yeah sure,' he said. 'Great idea, go ahead and become their next target,' he added sarcastically.

'Keira you are not to mention this to him or anyone,' he said solemnly.

'Fine, you have my word.'

★★★

The Vulnerable Side

'Hey there, wait,' called a student from behind as Keira walked past the economics section of the Bodleian Library that Sunday morning. 'Don't go there,' he cautioned, 'Cabir is sitting in the classics section and he doesn't like to be disturbed while he's working on something.'

Keira knew very well who he was talking about, yet she inquired, 'Cabir, who?'

'Cabir Dhawan,' he replied. 'Dare to bother him and he'll make sure you never forget that name,' he added and walked out.

With Steve and Sasha still having breakfast at the Great Hall, Keira decided to make the most of the opportunity and talk directly to Cabir so she walked towards the classics section instead.

'Hey,' she greeted Cabir who on this cold January morning sat in a denim blazer and blue jeans, next to a thick pile of books that Keira recognised to be from late antiquity.

'Hello Miss Malhotra,' he said as he raised his head to look at her. 'Come sit,' he offered pulling out a chair right next to him.

'You don't have to be so formal,' said Keira, taking a seat across the table even as she wondered why he was being so sweet to her when he was known to be ruthless with others.

Not knowing how to start the conversation, she started examining the books scattered on the table, surprised to find a *Harry Potter* book buried amidst his pile of classics.

'You've read it? Harry Potter?'

'Of course,' he said, 'this is one of the very first copies sold. You would know its worth if you were a...'

'Potterhead...,' they both said at the same time.

'Yeah,' he smiled, 'so have you been for some Harry Potter sightseeing yet?' he asked.

'Nah...but would love to go. Pretty soon hopefully...'

'All right I'll take you myself,' he smiled. Not knowing what to say, Keira smiled back.

'So what brings you here, Keira,' he asked seriously closing his book and looking into her eyes, 'What do you want?'

'I wanted to ask you something…' she hesitated.

'And what makes you think that I will give you an answer,' he asked bluntly. Keira had no answer, so he continued, 'I knew that my reputation would precede me. I assume Steve has told you his side of the story,' he correctly guessed. Keira sat confused wondering how he had suspected it.

'I want to hear your side of the story,' she mustered some courage and blurted.

'If no one has told you this Miss Malhotra, let me enlighten you myself. I don't give any kind of explanations, to anyone,' he asserted rudely.

'Yeah, but from what I have been told, you help no one; then why help me, and that too twice?' she demanded.

'Because I couldn't…' he was about to say something but stopped midway.

'You what Cabir?' Keira asked raising her voice. 'People say things about you but from what I have seen, you are not what they have made you to be.'

'You don't know me,' he barked but his voice sounded hurt, 'so don't be fooled coz I am a devil in disguise,' he said dismissing her words.

'We went away that day without finishing our conversation only to save you the trouble of seeing your friend's face getting smashed,' he said springing up.

'I won't back off, not anymore,' he declared. 'If only I had known you were friends with him I never would have…' He stopped abruptly and without even bothering to collect his books strode away from her.

'You would what!' Keira called from behind, perplexed at his weird behaviour. But he didn't turn and left without a word. She was stunned to witness this side of his character – the side that everyone was terrified of and her eyes welled up. Silenced by the librarian who had just arrived, she held back her tears as Cabir left the library banging the door much to the librarian's dismay.

'What is wrong with that boy?' Keira muttered to herself as she sat alone in the JCR that evening, waiting for Sasha and Steve who had gone to collect some study material.

She sat there talking to herself. For obvious reasons she could not discuss this with Steve. She herself did not understand how she had ended up in this mess. She hoped Steve hadn't encountered Cabir because if he had – one he would have a bleeding nose and two Keira would be in a bigger mess.

She still could not figure out why he behaved that

way. What had she said that made him so angry so suddenly? So what if she knew about what he had done to Steve and the others. He was the one who came to talk to her first so why dismiss her now. Cabir was like a puzzle with pieces that Keira wanted to fix together. He was right, she did not know his back-story and after the incident today, she tried her best to push him out of her mind and yet thoughts of him would crawl back in, his face popping up every few seconds. She just could not get rid of them.

'Keira, you won't believe what happened today,' exclaimed Sasha as they entered the JCR and took a seat next to her.

'I know right! No one in their right mind would,' Steve added his eyes shining with happiness. 'I am back in the football team and this time as a centre forward,' he announced proudly increasing Keira's confusion.

'Whoa, that's great,' she congratulated.

But if Cabir had been so desperate to keep him out how did he get in? she wondered. 'I don't understand. How did you manage to get back?' she asked.

'Well, that's the unbelievable part,' he narrated. 'This afternoon as I was walking back from class Mr Cabir Dhawan himself approached me, alone for a change,' he stressed and then reiterated what Cabir had said, 'what you did was wrong. However, I should not have taken it so far. I talked to the coach; you are back on the team; consult him this evening.'

'I must say the lad has got some contacts,' added Sasha.

'When I thanked him he said, "Thank your friend." and left,' Steve continued. 'Keira, Sasha doesn't know him. Do you happen to be his friend?' he asked looking at her suspiciously.

'I don't know Steve,' she said honestly, 'but what matters is that you are back on the team. Be happy and go meet the coach; it is almost time.'

'Yeah I should,' he agreed. 'Maybe Cabir isn't that bad after all,' he said and left to meet the coach.

Keira too decided to go back to the library to finish the task she was supposed to do that morning when Cabir and his unexpected behaviour had distracted her. Cabir yet again had done something that was unexpected of him. He somehow always managed to defy expectations; he would say something and then do something else. From what Keira had experienced, his actions hardly matched his words.

The next morning started with another deflection from Cabir's side, this time making Keira who had been trying to let go of the urge to confront him give in to the ardent feeling.

When she and Sasha got out of the room to attend the morning tuition session, Sasha found an envelope at their back door.

'A letter, that's funny,' she said picking up the envelope addressed to Keira. 'It is for you,' she said as she handed it over to her. Keira took it wondering who the sender was.

'You go on, I'll see you downstairs,' she told Sasha and opened the envelope, which contained a Hershey's bar and a white note, which she unfolded:

Keira,
I realise that I was rude to you yesterday. You have my apologies. You had after all just asked a question. I should not have acted as I did; my intention was not to hurt you.
I know Steve and I have had issues, but I have made an attempt to resolve it, just to make it up to you. As for your questions I will answer them when the time is right, which I predict will be soon.
Hoping to see you around,

Cabir

Determined to meet him in person she did not write a reply. However, she was not sure what she would say or ask when she did meet him but that was not to be a problem because soon news reached her that Cabir had got himself suspended, yet again, this time for a week and wasn't allowed to be seen on campus.

February is the shortest month of the year but with less daylight hours and absolutely no Cabir it felt like the longest. It was Valentines week. The snow had not started to melt yet.

That afternoon, the Great Hall was packed with people entering with their overcoats still on when Cabir Dhawan entered the hall, arrogant as ever and steered towards his friends' table.

Heads of pupils sitting at various tables turned to look at him as he walked past. Keira knew that his suspension was getting over today and was expecting him to show up. She had been looking out for him all day when he finally walked past the table where she sat with Sasha and Steve. A tiny shiver ran down her spine as she looked directly at him, and he looked back. But he didn't respond. There was not even a slight change in his expression as he kept on walking and reached his friends who got up to hug him after which they all took seats and began to talk among themselves.

Keira couldn't help but notice the peculiar way he looked through her as if she were just a stranger. She was looking right at his table when she saw him handing over a piece of paper to a stranger who turned and walked directly towards her table. Seeing him approach Keira looked away and pretended to focus on her meal. He came, kept the note next to her and went away.

She picked it up and read:

Come at four o'clock to end the quarrel where it began

Cabir

'What's this? asked Sasha who noticed that she was preoccupied.

'Nothing, just found something in my pocket,' Keira lied instantly. Thank God, Sasha had not seen Cabir giving it to the boy.

Keira looked at her watch. It was already 3:56 pm. She looked around to find that he had already vanished. That boy! He was always up to something. With Cabir Dhawan it was almost impossible to tell what would happen next, but maybe that is what excited her most about him.

Seeing no time left, she turned to Sasha and Steve, 'Guys I just remembered I have some urgent work in the library. I will see you people later in the common room,' she said and rushed towards the Bodleian.

Just when an already late Keira rushed out into the street, it began to snow. When she finally reached the classics section, she was covered in snow that started melting as soon as she entered the heated library making her damp.

She reached Cabir who stood exactly where they had met the last time. Standing there, sipping coffee from a takeaway mug, he smiled when she approached.

'Why are so…Achoo!' Keira sneezed, 'freaking unpredictable all…Achoo!'

'Look at you, all wet,' he shook his head in disapproval at her wet state. 'Come let's get you warmed up first.' He helped her remove her overcoat.

'Cabir, it's all right,' Keira said when he removed his own overcoat and wrapped it around her even as she was refusing it. 'Thanks,' she said already feeling better.

'Have this, it'll do you good,' he offered his coffee. Keira took a sip as he pulled chairs for both of them. 'So what would you like to know,' he questioned once she was warm and comfortable.

'Cabir,' she looked tenderly at him, 'I know I don't know much about you, but what I do know is that you make it difficult for anyone to understand you…'

'Understand me? What am I, some statistical data of yours?' He became angry again, which stunned Keira. 'Listen, Keira, I am sorry,' he amended immediately with a visible effort.

'I understand your concern – why does Cabir act the way he does? But believe me Keira, I am no angel drawn to the dark side or a devil who needs to be redeemed. There is just a trigger. I am trusting you with what I am about to tell you. Don't make me regret it,' he said placing his hands on the table and taking a deep breath.

'Have you heard of Zara S Dhawan?' he asked naming the well-known London socialite. Keira often saw her pictures in magazines.

'Yeah,' she replied. It had started to make some sense.

'She is my mother,' he stated.

'I didn't know she had a son!' she exclaimed, but Cabir's expression remained unchanged as if he'd expected the reaction.

'No one does. They never kept me with them, my parents. They were busy in their own worlds – mom with her charity balls, dad with his business and I in my impracticality kept dreaming of a life where we were all together.'

Finding it tough to express, he banged his hand on the table. He looked extremely vulnerable. Keira made a move to hold his trembling hand in hers. He didn't pull back but squeezed it hard as if gathering strength.

'Do you know what happens to a kid who gets dumped into a boarding school at the age of four; who is mocked by the children for not having any visitors or people to cheer him when he acts on stage or runs a race; who hardly ever goes home on holidays; whose parents aren't divorced but hardly ever see each other or come to see him, their mistake?' he asked.

His eyes welled up with tears but he managed to hold them back. He was always on guard, a guard that he never let down, not even when he narrated this tale of his, which probably came to define who he had become. He had been badly hurt. However like most people and yet in his own twisted way, he had learned to live with the wounds.

'Whatever may have happened to that kid, that kid sure as hell learnt this one thing,' he said as Keira listened to him in silence. 'In this world everyone is mean – everyone. If you don't fight you won't survive,' he added. His voice was shaking now. 'We all were fighting -- me, Kris, Veronica, Nate and Sid – and then we met each other. And we realised that we could fight anything if we were together.'

'We feared that we would break and that's why to win, to make sure that no one controls us...we...' He paused and looked into Keira's eyes and burst out, 'you want to know why I behave like I do, you want to know why we bully – we bully others, so that no one bullies us.'

'I have the best of friends, and I would do anything to protect them,' he added justifying his action against Steve and continued, 'And showing people who mess with my friends their proper place is one of them.'

'Keira, I really don't know why I am telling you this, I have never told anyone,' he admitted, running his other hand through his hair, making Keira aware that she still held the other one.

'That day, when I caught your camera, I wasn't meant to be on that bus. I was there to pick up Kris, but she had taken a taxi before I arrived…' he prattled something that didn't make much sense.

'I was about to leave when I saw you. You were there admiring the airport parking as if it were some marvel. You were looking all around with such eagerness that I couldn't resist following you. When you got into the bus, I climbed in after you. All through the journey – as you gawked at the streets, gazed at the stars and bent your head in obeisance when the bus crossed a cathedral – I just kept looking at you,' he said softly as she listened to him. She had been completely unaware of all this.

'You had this light about you, a light I had long lost as a child; and that light – it drew me to you. I know this is not exactly the era where people pull each other out of darkness; chances of darkness engulfing the light are more. But I wanted to know you,' he finally admitted. 'You should have met me in Middle School, you would have liked me too,' he ended.

Cabir seemed to be getting comfortable in being vulnerable around her. He wasn't shying away from confessing that he liked her.

'Hey, 'I like you even now,' she said in a whisper blushing furiously but Cabir didn't seem to be listening to her.

'I'll understand if you don't want to see me anymore,' he said not taking in her words, 'your friend doesn't like me and being seen with me isn't good for your reputation either,' he continued getting up slowly.

'Cabir, I do want to be your friend…I…' she protested but Cabir had already begun to walk away. 'At least take your coat,' she called out.

'You keep it Miss Malhotra,' he replied and walked out into the cold. That guy certainly didn't know how to end a conversation with a proper goodbye.

'So what do you want me to do? Lick their feet, beg them to give us that room,' screamed Mr Malhotra as the nuclear Malhotra family sat for dinner one night.

'Why are you overreacting, we just want our due

share in the property. We aren't asking for a favour,' Mrs Malhotra shouted back at her husband while the two kids, Manik and Keira listened with horrified expressions.

'How many times do we have to go through the same discussion? When will you get it straight? I don't want any share, I want to sell off this damned house and never look back,' Mr Malhotra retorted angrily.

'But…Dad…' Keira couldn't utter a single word further.

Every time this quarrel regarding the splitting of the Malhotra Mansion among the siblings – who could not even stand the sight of each other – came up the same routine followed. Mrs Malhotra would remind Keira that she was not going to live here for long. She would be off to college soon. It was they who would have to bear all the 'humiliation and injustice' at the hands of Mr Malhotra's prejudiced mother and predatory brother. For Keira it was no less than a 'No stay, so no say,' kind of situation.

'Mom, Dad,' interrupted little Manik, 'we don't want to leave, we love this house,' he pleaded as he turned to Keira, 'Keira, you tell them no, we want to live here.'

'Keira, haven't I told you, you are not to get your brother involved in this. He is a kid. Why do you brainwash him? How manipulative can you get?' Mrs Malhotra diverted her anger towards Keira who did not speak a word in response.

'Mom she didn't say anything,' protested Manik.

'Oh, shut up you two, go to your room! Keira you better make sure I don't hear a word about this again,' he ordered as the kids left the dining hall and the couple continued to fight on top of their voices.

★★★

The Revelation

'Keira!' called Sasha, shaking her arm as they sat in the dining hall that night, 'Keira, where are you? What's wrong?'

'Nothing,' she said and pulled herself together as she recovered from the flashback of her family who repeatedly fought over a house that meant more to Keira than anyone else. Cabir's confession about his family had taken her back. Here at Oxford she had been sheltered from the quarrels and the tensions. But the truth was that her family – just like Cabir's and those of so many others – had problems which at every other step bothered her, affected her in ways which weren't always visible only felt.

'Keira, you can do it in the morning,' suggested Sasha, when Keira told her that she would be staying up most of the night to write the vote appeal speech she had to make to the panel of voters in the coming weekend.

It was the last week before the term ended. With the end of February arriving, the snow had started to melt and spring didn't seem far away.

'Nah, I ought to get it done tonight. I can't concentrate in daylight,' she replied.

Throughout the day, she was preoccupied searching for Cabir, who she had not seen since that day in the library: Her eyes kept wandering as she sat for meals, walked the streets or went to the common rooms; he was nowhere to be seen. She was extremely distracted.

It was Sasha who found out that he had gone to attend a confidential court hearing in Delhi, which made Keira more concerned than she'd anticipated.

The clock had already stuck 3 am when she finished the speech. She would read it to Sasha and Steve tomorrow for editing. Tired and sleepy, she got up, stretched her arms and yawned; hungry she put cup noodles on the induction and waited. Glancing out of the window, she was astonished to see a tall boy, dressed in black staring at the lake. His back was turned towards her building and a red convertible was parked at the gate. The boy stood still for a while lost in thought as Keira kept looking at him.

Then he bent down, ran his hands through his hair as if gathering strength and stood up erect the next second. It was when he finally turned and looked up through the length of the building with puppy eyes that Keira's heart raced as she recognized Cabir, standing at the entrance of her hostel in the middle of the night, when everyone else thought he was out of the country.

At once Keira turned off the induction, wore her overcoat and headed downstairs to check on him because no normal person would behave this way at 3:15 in the night.

Perhaps he had heard her coming down, for when she reached the ground floor he was staring at the door as if expecting someone.

'Cabir!' she exclaimed, when she saw him. He was in his travelling attire, his eyes were exhausted, his face miserable. 'Cabir, are you all right? What's wrong?' She freaked out when he didn't respond for a moment and kept staring at her.

'Has it ever happened to you...' he said coming closer as Keira walked towards him, '...you get a shock and feel like your mind is going to explode?'

But before she could even contemplate an answer Cabir leaned forward, and in a very unexpected gesture wrapped his arms around her shoulders, and pulled her close for a tight hug. Startled at the sudden closeness Keira felt many emotions swirling in her heart; she too responded moving one arm around his waist and the other arm gently caressing his back offering comfort. His arms squeezed a fraction tighter, his muscles relaxed and he closed his eyes and breathed slowly, finding solace in the arms of a girl, he had not even exchanged phone numbers with.

A few seconds later Cabir realized what he had done. Overwhelmed with emotions he had instinctively looked to her for comfort but now with realization came awareness. He loosened his grip and started moving away.

'Listen, wait!' Keira called from behind as he strode towards his parked car but he did not stop. He got in and was about to start the car when Keira exclaimed with exasperation, 'Cabir, how will I know what has happened if you don't tell me?'

'Forget it, I shouldn't have come,' he said regretfully as he sunk his head into his hands.

'But now that you have...' she said as she tried to make him sit up, 'talk to me, whatever is in your head spit it out. Tell me,' she pleaded, his behaviour making her anxious.

Uncertain of his next move he flung open the car door, missing hitting Keira by inches. He stood with his hands on his waist, and looked at her in two minds. 'I...I don't know...Why is it...' he breathed deeply. 'Cabir calm down. It's ok, you are ok,' he murmured to himself.

'Come here, sit down,' suggested Keira, putting her hands on his drooping shoulders. They moved to the nearest bench.

'My mom and dad – they finally got divorced,' he said in a wounded voice. 'I went to Delhi as I was a witness,' he said in a low voice. 'I am twenty so neither of them got custody, though dad has been instructed to send me a big fat check every month,' he said straightening himself up a bit before disclosing the final shocker…'and as we came out of the court Zara declared that she was getting married,' he paused to let the words sink in.

'We were never a big happy family. For her I have only been a means to get money from dad. She won't need me any longer now that she's marrying that British investment banker,' he said sadly.

'It may seem silly or childlike, but I don't want a stepdad…Today was her engagement…I didn't attend it. I booked my ticket and came back here…' He stopped to rub his eyes trying to stem the tears which threatened to spill over as Keira held his other hand.

'It is not childish Cabir, it is natural. You are their child. You were not ready for this and it makes you unhappy,' she said.

'The whole situation is new for you. It is natural to be upset. But if you give it some time, try to understand them; then it won't seem so difficult. Familiarize yourself with the new changes, and you'll see everything will be all right,' she tried to reassure him but he shook his head hopelessly.

'There is nothing to understand Keira. My parents – they went their separate ways, leaving me alone with a trust fund,' he complained.

'Cabir, you are not alone. I am here for you, your friends are here,' she consoled even as her eyes began to tear up seeing him so heartbroken. His guards were down. He was so upset and mad at the latest occurrence that it seemed as if he had succumbed to the grief.

'When you're a little kid learning to paddle you tend to fall a lot. But you know that there are people watching your back, people who will catch you and won't let you fall,' he said. 'But when I fell there was no one to protect me and so I kept on falling until I reached a state where I stopped feeling pain anymore; the hard earth couldn't hurt me anymore. They have made me what I am today,' he concluded.

'And what are you?'

'Don't pretend Keira, I know what I have become; someone who my childhood self – who always wanted to play the hero – would never approve of,' he said trying to laugh it off.

'Cabir listen to me,' she said seriously. 'People are not bad, their situations are. You are a good person to whom this bad thing has happened,' she said quoting *Sirius Black.*

'Keira, thank you,' he said earnestly. 'I don't know how I landed up here. I had decided not to see you again, at least not until the elections were over,' he said trying to understand his unnatural behaviour. 'One moment I was at the arrivals at the Heathrow International Airport, not knowing what to do, where to go and the next moment I was driving all the way here…to you…Why?' he said, burying his head in her hands.

'How would I know?' She blushed sensing the emerging feelings.

'This kind of conversation doesn't happen with any of my friends, but I spit it all out to you, so easily, you are different,' he said.

'Is there anything wrong with me? she laughingly asked.

'I'm the one who has made you sit on a park bench at four in the morning, and you think there's something wrong with you,' he finally pulled off a smile.

'Do you want to come up and maybe eat something,' she offered now that he appeared to be better.

'Nah…It is the girls hostel. I should go.'

'No…You need to eat. You stay right here. I'll be back. Don't move,' she instructed. He didn't argue.

A soft tickle ran down Keira's chest as she climbed up

the stairs knowing that Cabir was waiting for her. Maybe she'd started to understand Cabir, maybe he wasn't that complex after all, just human. Like most people we encounter in our life, he too had faced inevitable suffering brought about by harsh changes in his life which had probably made him adopt a different outlook towards life. Such situations often make us either anxious or rebellious. He had chosen to be the latter. The doubts she had about him began to vanish like stars in the morning sky. He was like a nut – hard and firm from the outside and yet yearning to be that sensitive hero on the inside.

Keira returned ten minutes later with two cups of noodles and his overcoat, which had been with her for half the winter.

She walked towards him. She found him lost in thought sitting in the same position she'd left him in, gazing at the stars that twinkled in the twilight.

'Do you like the stars?' she asked, handing over the cup from which he took a spoonful.

'I used to. I noticed you like them,' he guessed accurately.

'Yeah, I love them. They appear so tiny in the night sky and yet manage to overcome the darkness and shine,' she mused. 'Not to forget they're the reason I'm here with you.'

'What?'

'Cabir, haven't you ever wondered why some things happen in a certain way and not the other way round?' she asked.

When he seemed confused, she continued, 'My grandma often used to say to me that the outline of our life is already drawn, like an outer boundary of a house, and it is up to us to fill the space it encloses with things that make it worthwhile.'

'I don't get you.'

'I mean, it's like the stars have blessed every one of us with a canvas but what we paint on it, is up to us,' she explained, 'I know our life at this point is not really a blank canvas anymore but at least we can always repaint over the dull colours with colours that make us happy.'

'Okay...so all of us have the *blessing of stars...* fascinating...' he said gazing heavenwards. They spent the next couple of minutes watching the constellations as Keira pointed them out.

'Hey, good morning,' whispered Cabir when Keira opened her eyes after an unplanned nap. Weary after a long day, she had dozed off as they gazed at the stars. Now waking up after a quarter of an hour, she found herself lying partially in Cabir's arms covered with the overcoat she had just returned. He had wrapped it around her to shield her from the cold while he sat still with his arms wrapped around her.

'What time is it? I don't know how I fell asleep,' she said, straightening herself up a bit as he kept looking at her.

'Around 5,' he said, 'you looked so peaceful sleeping I couldn't disturb you.'

'Cabir, go home. Get some rest; you need it,' she seemed genuinely concerned on seeing his exhausted eyes. She got up to her feet.

'Keira, I know most people like being left alone when distressed,' he said uncurling himself, 'but for me...if I had been alone yesterday it wouldn't have gone very well, so thank you for bearing with me.'

She smiled, seeing that his mood seemed to have lifted up a bit.

'And yes Keira Malhotra,' he said as he was about to get into his car, 'I am all right. Don't worry about me.'

'Oh…I don't,' she denied.

'I know you do,' he said as he got into his car and within seconds drove out of sight.

'How're you holding up?' Keira asked Cabir the next day when she saw him sitting in the Cathedral ground constantly scribbling on a notepad.

'Never better,' he said looking up, his expression dismissing any scope for continuing the previous night's conversation. With his guard up again, he clearly didn't want to converse about his family and so Keira didn't bring it up either and sat across him.

'What are you writing?'

'Ah…' He put down his pen. 'Mrs Wade wants us to write a feminist story with a modern approach. And being a writer of romanticism I am having a bit of trouble, writers block rather,' he explained.

'Well maybe I can help you out,' she offered, '*FYI* I'm a born feminist,' she declared.

'And I'll be more than grateful for this help,' he said in a mildly mocking tone.

'So tell me, have you thought of something, anything till now?'

'Well, there are these fairy tales I've come across. In fact the only girly stories I have ever come across are the ones where there is a pretty princess who is in grave trouble and sings for a prince to come rescue her and give her a happily ever after,' he narrated the plot of most fairy tales.

'And that is exactly what needs to be altered,' she beamed as an idea took shape in her mind. 'Did you notice girls are always portrayed as needing some strong prince to come and save them,' she pointed out. 'But why do they need a prince? Can't they save themselves or maybe the prince himself?'

'Well that is not happening.'

'Think about it Cabir, when a mother narrates a fairy tale to her daughter, she manages to ignite a certain hope within her that someday a prince charming or whoever would come rescue her from the big bad world and change her life – and that is what is so not happening,' she contradicted.

'I get it now!' Cabir loved the idea, 'You're a genius Keira and here I thought I was the writer.' He was thrilled.

'Hey Cabir!' called Sid from a few meters away, 'Don't you have a class to attend?' Cabir began gathering his stuff.

'Coming…' he responded and then turned to Keira, 'Got to go right now Miss Malhotra. You are amazing,' he said and kissed her lightly on her left cheek leaving her stunned. He got up and rushed to Sid and the two of them sprinted towards the classroom.

***

The Astonishing Decider

Winter winds had blown past and summer was just around the corner when the students of Oxford University came back for the Trinity Term in April.

The atmosphere was brimming with election buzz and gossip as it was to be held in the very first weekend, giving the candidates including Keira and her rival Lucas very less time to campaign and gain last moment allies.

The week had been an exceptionally tiring one for Keira as she toured JCR's with her friends gathering support and stayed up through the nights covering up for classes she'd skipped. Thoughts of Cabir often did cross her mind but going to meet him or find out about his rather unknown whereabouts had taken a backseat in her schedule of things to do.

'I don't know what's going to happen,' she told Sasha and Steve who had been waiting for her on one of the wings of the stage as she came back after presenting a vote appeal and introducing her agenda in front of the voters. They would be casting their votes that evening. 'I am not sure about anything,' she said nervously.

'Well, I am certain about one thing after today,' Sasha rolled her eyes towards Cabir who was standing at the back of the auditorium constantly looking in their direction. He smiled when Keira looked at him and she smiled back.

'What?' she asked, not noticing that they had noticed her exchanging smiles with the crass Cabir Dhawan.

'That Cabir couldn't take his eyes off you,' she declared as Keira somehow managed to hold back the blush that was spreading on her cheeks. 'C'mon Keira, what is the fun of having a crush when you can't tell your best friend about him!'

'What!' exclaimed Steve in disbelief.

'Oh…I have to rush backstage,' she said in order to avoid answering. 'We have to stay with the other candidates till the voting is done.' She made up an excuse and left within seconds resolving in her mind that she would tell Steve next week when things slowed down a bit.

'Keira, look what I found,' said Sasha waving an

envelope she had found at the door while returning from dinner, 'It is a letter – another one!'

'I really don't care about any letter,' Keira replied as she paced the room getting more anxious as night drew. She was waiting for the morning hour when the results would be announced, '…Unless it is the one confirming my winning the election.'

'Keira, I mean it's **a letter**!!!' she teased, reminding Keira of the one person who was likely to write to her. 'It's for you,' Sasha said confirming her guess as she handed it over and Keira silently read:

> Dear Keira
> I know you must be pacing your room with butterflies fluttering in your stomach, butterflies eager to fly high tomorrow. Trust me that is common. However, what is not common is you. And this election is not even a quarter of what your stars have blessed you with. All you have to do tonight is believe and yeah have this chocolate bar before you try to catch some sleep. All right Miss Malhotra?
> If you need my help for anything, I am just a text away.
> Eagerly waiting for the treat you'll be giving tomorrow.
>
> Cabir

That night as Sasha lay fast asleep; Keira lay on her bed wide-awake, wondering what tomorrow would bring. Cabir Dhawan – she wondered why he thought so highly of her, at a time when not many and perhaps even she didn't. In that moment even though he was not around, his words gave her a boost and hope; and in that moment, she adored him.

'All right Cabir, I believe you,' she said to herself as she took a bite of the Hershey's bar he'd put in the envelope along with the letter.

Keira skipped breakfast that morning and dressed in formals to attend the result declaration ceremony. She took a deep breath, clenched her hands and entered the hall where people had begun to assemble.

She took her place among the other nominees who sat in rows of chairs placed in the front near the podium. Lucas who sat three spaces before her gave a scornful grin as she looked past him to see the announcer who had now arrived at the stage.

She couldn't hear the announcer for her own heartbeat was louder than the mike. She glanced at the crowd to see a few familiar faces amidst who were the happy ones of Sasha and Steve and that of Cabir who as usual had made a fashionably late entrance in the hall. He sat in the last row along with his friends and smiled widely at her when their eyes met for a second.

The names of the treasurer and a few vice presidents were announced. Now it was the turn for vice president women. It could be any moment now – she could be proved wrong or many others could be proved wrong.

'...Keira Malhotra,' she heard her name announced. She had won.

Finally, a victory after the many defeats she had suffered. She didn't scream joyfully or shed tears of happiness. For a moment, she didn't feel a thing. An ocean of memories flashed in front of her eyes and rattled her ears instead of the cheering of the people who had come to support her. All that criticism she had buried inside came rushing to pull her down as she got up.

'Keira do you really feel you have it in you: to be elected in a student's union that too at Oxford. You need to mend that attitude of yours if you are to reach anywhere,' Mrs Malhotra's chastisement – when she informed her parents about her nomination – echoed in her ears.

'Are you popular enough that people will vote for you? Aren't there people who are better than you are?' Mr Malhotra's doubts too crept in along with the criticism that flowed in her mind as she walked towards the podium.

And amidst all these voices overlapping in her mind one stood out, which didn't question her, which didn't doubt her – 'Today is your day Miss Malhotra. You'll get what you want.' The voice was Cabir's. It overpowered the others. She knew what she felt for him was more than just a crush.

She blindly made her way to the podium lost in a storm of thoughts, so she didn't see the crowd applauding or hear their hoots. She was completely unaware of the strangers who clapped for her, her friends, who were thrilled and the others who were not. However, for her it didn't matter who cheered and who didn't, for in that moment the one person who mattered the most was content – she herself.

'Getting a bit emotional, are we?' the commentator teased kindly seeing her emotional state. Mr Dippet came forward to hand over her badge after which she was directed to the podium to take her oath as the vice president–women.

'I promise to fulfil all the duties and responsibilities assigned to me with the best of my ability and uphold the Oxford flag...'

'You nailed it Keira, you did it!' Sasha jumped to hug her when she reached backstage after receiving greetings from what felt like the hundredth person.

'You should have seen Lucas's face when **your** name was announced,' Steve bragged as he hugged her too.

'We need to celebrate *ASAP*,' declared Sasha as they decided to head to *Victor's* café and bar for lunch.

'You guys head there, look at the menus and I'll see you in ten minutes, Keira said. 'I just need some alone time to let it all sink in,' she said smiling brightly.

The minute they left, she let the tears flow. She had been holding them back with great difficulty as a mix of varied emotions churned within her.

'Do I need to say that I knew you'll win?' came Cabir's voice as he appeared backstage unannounced. 'Congratulations Miss Malhotra,' he said extending a hand, which Keira didn't take. Instead, she gave in to her instinct and hugged him. He hesitated for a moment, and then returned the gesture.

'You don't know how much your letter, how much all of this means to me,' she confessed as she broke away.

'Actually I do,' he said. 'These, clearly reflect how much it means to you,' he said pointing to the tears that had wet her face.

'Cabir I don't know how I can ever thank you enough,' she said wiping off the leftover traces of the tears which were a testament to how thrilled she was.

'I know how,' he teased by slightly bending his cheek towards her indicating a kiss.

'Listen Keira …' Sasha appeared, out of the blue, just when Keira was about to decide whether to comply or shy away, 'oh …sorry to interrupt you guys,' she smiled teasingly.

'No, it's absolutely fine,' Keira said stepping back from Cabir who seemed equally startled and didn't know how to react.

'My friends, the people from the club too are demanding a treat. Do you mind if they join us?' she asked hopefully.

'Oh, not at all,' Keira replied, 'the more the merrier.'

'Great,' Sasha's face lit up, 'I'll go inform them and leave you guys to do whatever it was you were about to do,' she winked at Keira and walked out.

'Your friend has perfect timing,' muttered Cabir as they stood through five seconds of awkward silence while Sasha made her way out.

'Cabir, we were all going to celebrate at Victor's. I would like it very much if you and your friends join us,' she invited him.

'Sure,' he agreed after considering the offer.

'I'll see you there then,' Keira smiled at him as they walked in opposite directions for now, only to meet in time.

'To the girl of the hour,' Sasha raised a toast, as the group of newly found acquaintances joined in with their respective glasses of beer while all of them sat in Victor's that afternoon.

'I know it's all light,' Sasha commented as she took a sip, 'but no worries, since it is the big win of my girl, we'll toast with something which isn't light at night,' her announcement was followed by a cheer.

Everything was going fine like any normal get together until all of a sudden some people began to look uneasy; a few of them got up and bid farewell as they attempted to get out of their seats.

'What the hell are they doing here?' said Steve equally uneasy. Keira turned around to see what was causing this sudden interruption in her luncheon, 'Since when did this coffee shop become the hangout of this hi-fi gang?' he said disgusted as Cabir and his friends walked into Victor's arrogantly, as if they were there to witness a street fight.

'Sasha, I completely forgot about their rift,' Keira owned up turning to her as the gang walked directly towards their table, 'I invited them!' she whispered.

'You didn't!' she exclaimed, 'What were you thinking!'

Before she could answer, Cabir announced himself at the table.

'Hello guys,' he said in a voice that was more brusque than what he used with Keira, 'there isn't a need to leave so soon, is there?' he said addressing the people who got up at his arrival. 'Come sit down,' he offered, and even though they were puzzled at the unexpected politeness, everyone obeyed.

'Hey Steve,' Veronica called out making Steve jump at the unexpected greeting, 'would you mind coming outside with me for a moment?' she asked as the others took their seats.

'Why? Do you want to beat me up now?' he asked crossly.

'No honey, I wanted a word, in private,' she said seductively, placing her hand on his shoulder. Steve got up and followed without a word.

'But Steve…what?' yelled Sasha as he got up and left with her potential rival.

'No one will pay today, all day,' Cabir announced as the waiters appeared to take orders. 'Today's treat is from me, for this wonderful, wonderful girl,' he said raising his glass to Keira as she turned to him in amazement.

'Cabir, there was no need for any of this,' Keira said.

'Yes there was,' he said in a tone that put a stop to all further debate.

'Fine,' she said and let it go. 'You are not going to do anything to Steve, are you?' she asked.

'Of course not, he's your friend. He's going to be more than all right, you'll see,' he said reassuring her.

'Cabir, I am very curious to know how a tall guy like you managed to slide those letters through our door,' said Sasha interrupting them.

'Which letters?' he asked faking ignorance.

'I know you like Keira,' she said straightaway as he smiled in the most adorable manner, 'but letters in this era of DM's!'

'Well I just think that letters carry more warmth than any text message,' he said, 'Don't they Keira?'

'Yes, they do.'

'Of course they would, if such a ridiculously hot guy wrote them,' she grinned. Cabir smirked in response and Keira's expression said: **Don't flirt with him!**

'Cabir, I know you are here for my girl but if you continue with that stupid sexy smirk of yours it is me who's going to fall for you instead, and we all know it isn't me who you want,' she smirked back.

Suddenly there was an awkward pause in the conversation, which was cut short when Steve and Veronica returned holding each other's hands. Veronica was blushing and Steve looked as if he had won a million dollar lottery.

'Attention guys,' he said loudly perhaps trying to adopt Cabir's manner of greeting, 'Me and Veronica here…we're officially dating,' he announced proudly as Veronica stood on her toes and gave him a kiss. This was followed by an applause from the crowd at Victor's and a 'what the…' reaction from Sasha and Keira.

'How on earth did you do that?' Keira questioned Cabir while everyone was busy eating.

'What makes you so sure that I had anything to do with that?' he parried.

'I doubt Veronica would have made such a move without seeking advice from your gang,' she stated the evident. 'As for my friend – it doesn't seem as if he would care for any advice from his friends,' she added sarcastically.

'Patience Miss Malhotra, you will get to know the whole story from Steve himself,' he said without refuting his involvement, 'I don't want to spoil his fun,' he smirked as Keira got up all annoyed and walked towards the counter while he sat there gawking.

'Keira – she must be special,' commented Sid who had been sitting quiet all this time, observing the brand new PDA (public display of affection) of the new 'couple' and whatever chit chat was happening between his best mate and the newly elected representative of his college.

'Why would you say that?' Cabir asked without showing any change in his expression.

'You care about only a few people; it is hard to miss when you do,' he said as he got up to leave having finished his meal, leaving the bossy and tough Cabir Dhawan tongue-tied.

'We are going to leave too,' declared Steve when the waiters started collecting the empty plates. He and Veronica made their way out of the café into one of the not so crowded streets for yet another session of PDA.

'Sasha, is it?' Cabir attempted to initiate a conversation with Sasha who seemed to be preoccupied staring at the two love birds as they exited from the cafe. There was a longing on her face, a longing for something that Steve had just found today. Cabir recognized that feeling in her because he himself had longed for many things in life he never had.

'I'm sorry,' he said genuinely when Sasha turned around on hearing her name being called, 'I might have prevented this from happening, if only I knew before that you had a thing for Steve.'

'How do you know?' she asked; though she didn't deny the fact, she was rather taken aback when she realized that he was aware of it.

'The way you looked at the two of them today, I guess everyone came to know except for that jerk,' he said referring to her not so usual behaviour upon seeing the two together – the manner in which she tried to control her feelings from taking over her face – how she attempted to act normal when the two headed out hand in hand.

'Now if you'd excuse me,' she sprang to her feet without any further questions. 'And Cabir, you should hang around often if you want to have Keira,' she advised, 'or you can still have me, if not her,' she made her way out with her final wink for the afternoon, for even when in pain and anguish Sasha wasn't Sasha without a bit of sass.

'I knew you wouldn't give in so easily,' Cabir commented when he walked up to the counter and caught Keira red-handed trying to pay the bills herself. 'I am a regular customer with an account here therefore all your attempts are in vain for the lunch has already been paid for,' he said.

'All right, you pay,' Keira said accepting defeat in that battle but immediately picking up another fight, 'But I want to know when you will stop scaring people to such an extent that they have to get up and leave when you arrive,' she asked expressing her contempt for his practice of frightening people off.

'When you assure me that they won't start scaring me if I stop scaring them,' he said.

'You're way too complicated,' she chuckled as she turned around to leave, 'I want to see you sorted out.'

'And you are happy today,' he said pulling her back. 'I want to see you this happy every day,' he whispered into her ear making it tickle before he let her go.

'Like seriously!' exploded Sasha back in the common room when they finally met with Steve the next morning,

'One day you're bitching about how she's such a nasty mean girl and the next day she becomes "your girl" and then you go on and on..."oh Veronica's so nice, she's so pretty,"' she imitated Steve.

'Sasha what is wrong with you?' he demanded as though he didn't have any idea; then perhaps he didn't.

'What's wrong is you being with her...' she yelled at him and stopped abruptly. The sentence would have made more sense if she had added '*and not me*' to it.

'I like her, she likes me; in fact Keira, you won't believe this...' He started narrating the happenings which resulted in his grin and Sasha's frown. 'When Veronica took me outside she began by apologising for all the trouble she and Cabir had caused,' he emphasized on it because he knew how big a deal an apology was for Cabir and company.

'She said she fancied me. Can you imagine the hottest girl in college fancies me,' he said with an idiotic grin. Once she apologized and now that there was no trouble between her friends and me, she asked me out,' he sighed.

'And I wonder what your answer would have been,' interrupted Sasha, who appeared to be as disinterested in Steve's story as one is in a Principal's lecture.

'Yes, I agreed,' he ignored her, 'as if I would have said no to her.'

'Whatever...if you're happy then I'm happy for you,' said Keira.

'I wish I could say the same,' murmured Sasha under her breath, in a voice so low that no one could hear.

Then she pulled herself together and in her usual flamboyant way said, 'I too have a bottom line analysis.'

'And what would that be?' Steve asked unsmilingly, extending their cold war, which had begun the previous afternoon and Keira wondered would continue for how long.

'The next time anyone raises a toast to all the single people in the house I'll be the only one drinking to it,' she forced a chuckle, 'now that even this idiot has found a girlfriend.' She threw him a nasty glare. 'Keira, you have got to find some hot guy for me, or I'll be the only single person left in this room.'

'Hey, I am single,' stated Keira

'Yes of course,' she teased, '…and absolutely ready to mingle.'

'No,' said her tongue, *maybe* said her heart.

★★★

All Smiles, Some Tears & Little Fears

'And then the princess found herself locked in a tall tower which was surrounded by a moat filled with crocodiles and guarded by a fire emitting dragon.' The mother was reading a bedtime story to her darling daughter. She made a pitiful face and continued , 'the poor princess stayed locked for weeks and waited for Prince Charming all through the day and night…,' she read when the little girl interrupted .

'But mom, why is the princess waiting for a prince?' she innocently asked.

'To save her, silly,' the mother stated the obvious reason.

'But why does she need a prince to save her mommy,' she argued. 'If I were in her place I would have used all that time to tame the dragon and flown away on its back and saved myself on my own,' she stated confidently. 'This princess is silly!' she declared and pushed away the book

> of fairy tales from her mother's hands.
> 'Well, I guess it's time we rewrite our fairy tales,' the mother, who was dumbstruck by her daughter's courage, said as she kissed her goodnight.

Cabir Dhawan narrated to his class one morning.

Everyone clapped as he paused to catch a breath and then continued, 'Someone special recently reminded me that you don't need to be a female to be a feminist; for feminism is something which makes you a true man.'

'For most of us guys in here, it is our mothers who have taught us to be responsible, independent, brave and strong. However, what we should never forget is that the very woman, who made us so, possesses each and every one of these traits within her,' he said with conviction.

'They are just a bit hidden beneath the blanket of patriarchy we've forced upon them. Not wanting to take more of your time, let me clarify this; don't live in this fantasy that a girl is incomplete without you for she is the one without whom you'll be paralysed. She doesn't need your help or your permission, all she needs is for you to stop being a pebble in her path and let her soar,' he said sincerely and concluded. The class broke into a spontaneous applause.

'To the girl, who made a nincompoop like me believe in all that I said,' he added dedicating his writing to Keira, who he had invited as a guest to witness his classroom reading. 'Keira Malhotra,' he announced as he looked towards Keira who sat in one of the chairs in the last row.

The eye of every person sitting in that room followed Cabir's gaze and faces turned to look at Keira and acknowledge her with another round of applause as she too humbly stood up and gently smiled to thank all of them.

'So how was it?' inquired Cabir as he reached up to Keira at the end of the class.

'Mrs Wade seemed to be very happy,' replied Keira.

'What about you?'

'I am happy,' she smiled at him as they headed out into the corridor, 'I never knew that a boy could give such a moving speech about women,' she said. 'No one does that – what you did today Cabir; and I am so proud.'

And then she took the courage to lean closer and reward his cheek with a kiss startling him completely. 'What was that for?' he blushed.

'You deserve it, you really do,' she answered, 'coz no one has ever made me feel this worthwhile,' she confessed.

'Aw…how sweet,' mocked Lucas as he walked past the two of them in the corridor, 'you two should definitely try out for the summer love contest this semester.' He laughed.

'I really don't remember asking for your damn advice,' Cabir called him out as he took a step away from Keira, instantly transforming from a gentleman into a fearful monster and grabbed Lucas by his collar.

Within a blink of an eye, the verbal argument turned into a boxing match with Cabir breaking Lucas' nose with the very first punch. Lucas groaned but it didn't stop him. He also fought back viciously. He lashed at him with an elbow to his chest; Cabir flinched but went on to squeeze his face before taking a shot at his jaws. Lucas punched Cabir in the chest as he tried to push him back, Cabir retaliated by slapping his face as he grabbed his neck like a pro wrestling champion.

The two fought like bloodthirsty enemies with Keira desperately trying to stop them. A crowd of people passing by gathered around to witness the fight. The fight finally ended when a few of them intervened and pulled them apart even as they struggled to get back at each other.

'This isn't over yet,' shouted Cabir as they dragged Lucas away from his reach. 'You're going to suffer real badly; I'll make sure of it!' he threatened as he was left standing beside Keira while the crowd resumed their activities.

Witnessing this side of Cabir, which everyone but she was familiar with left Keira shocked and terrified but she gathered herself to calm him down.

'Cabir are you all right?' she asked fearfully as he breathed heavily, his face full of sweat, his collar bone bruised and his knuckles dripping blood on the floor. But he didn't seem to react or show signs of pain even as they tottered to the nearest park bench.

'Sit down Cabir,' she ordered and he obeyed only now becoming aware of his bleeding hand, '...and breathe all right.'

'You need to calm down and get a grip on yourself,' she said grabbing a water bottle and a handkerchief from her handbag. 'This may hurt a bit,' she warned as she took his hand into hers and dabbed the wet handkerchief on the fresh wounds.

'I am used to it.' He appeared to have taken control of his fuming rage as she cleaned up the blood. He winced at her ministrations. 'You may want to fold it diagonally and then tie it,' he suggested as she struggled to wrap the handkerchief across his knuckles.

'When did you become such a doctor?' She smiled as she followed his instruction.

'You learn to take care of yourself when you keep getting into all these fights,' he smiled back when she finished the dressing.

'It is going to be just fine,' she assured him as she bent down to kiss the handkerchief which she had wrapped around his knuckles, 'But, why Cabir?' she finally asked what she had been meaning to all this time, 'Why do you keep getting into these fights?'

'I like to stand up for my friends,' he replied simply, 'I told you I'm always ready to hurt anyone who messes around with them.'

'Cabir, but it isn't only they who get hurt, I mean just look at you,' she said pointing at his injured hand.

'If it's for my friends then I don't mind getting hurt,' he said adamantly.

'Did he do something to you guys? Lucas? she asked even though she didn't know if she was entitled to an answer. 'This is the third time I've seen you pounce on him.'

'Fine, I'll tell you,' he surprisingly responded, 'But you shouldn't tell Steve, Veronica will, if she feels like,' he put forth a condition to which Keira agreed.

'Lucas is Veronica's ex,' he explained. 'They dated for about a year before she literally caught him cheating on her at the start of last semester. She was really into him and was shattered when they broke up,' he said in a voice filled with anger and vengeance. 'She distanced herself from everybody, even us. There was nothing we could do except making his life a living hell and so we did. You cannot go after the people who are important to me and leave without a mark.'

'Now that she's with Steve, is she over him?' Concern

for Steve made Keira ask the question.

'I hope so,' he replied, 'I remember her coming to us one day and saying that she was interested in this guy on my football team. Then she got offended when he flirted with her, and I being myself went after him,' he said explaining his actions against Steve.

'If you were so sure that Steve was wrong for her, then what made you change your mind Cabir?'

'You,' he admitted, 'I changed my mind when I got to know that he was your friend, I knew then he couldn't possibly be that bad.'

'And you were right,' she said. 'So how about you? Any awkward exes?' she asked.

'Yeah, I dated this girl back in high school. It wasn't serious though. I mean, can you imagine Cabir Dhawan going to the movies, holding hands, carrying roses. Just wouldn't suit my image,' he joked, 'We went separate ways but nothing awkward you know.'

'I wouldn't know,' she admitted, 'I don't have any ex.'

'Seriously!' he was amused. 'So you are not seeing anyone right now and you don't have an ex...' he calculated, 'That means you haven't had a boyfriend in eighteen long years,' he exclaimed as though it was the most unnatural thing.

'Whatever!'

'You need to come with me.' He leaped up at once and

offered her his uninjured hand to pull her up. 'I have got to give you something,' he said and without saying anything more, he directed her toward the Radcliffe Camera.

'*Romeo and Juliet*!' exclaimed Sasha when to her surprise she found Keira reading a book which was clearly out of her course.

'Cabir gave it to me,' she responded as she placed a bookmark on the fourth scene.

'Did he now?' Steve asked pointedly. He still wasn't a great fan of Mr Dhawan.

'A guy gave you *Romeo and Juliet*, not bad Keira,' Sasha teased, 'what other sign do you need?'

'What is the deal with you and Cabir?' Steve asked bluntly.

'There is no deal,' Keira responded instantly. 'He knew I hadn't read it and wanted me to read it. That's it.'

'Cabir, the way he behaves around you, it's just not him. I mean compared to the way he is with others,' Steve commented.

'No it isn't!'

'Anyways, I don't think he is the kind of person, who believes in promising the moon and stars to his beloved.' Sasha came to her rescue by diverting the discussion from the route it was heading towards.

'Do tell me if anyone ever manages to fulfil that promise,' joked Steve.

'Well, if you consider it,' said Keira, 'there are organisations through which you can actually get a star registered in the name of someone you love.'

'All right forgive me,' laughed Steve, 'But whatever you guys say, love hardly has any value left nowadays,' he continued, 'there isn't much difference between "*I love your shoes*" and "*I love you*".'

'Then how will I know if it is really *love*?' Sasha asked.

'I guess when you're in love, you just know,' Keira replied.

During the next two weeks of the semester Cabir's group and Keira along with Steve and Sasha spent more time hanging out together – going to cafes, attending the guys' footballs matches and sitting together in the Great Hall. This allowed Veronica and Steve to spend more time with one another and also Cabir and Keira who enjoyed each other's company.

Keira was very busy with her student union duty calls and Cabir with his endless list of essays. But they would still find time to text each other. They would talk every other night via direct messages. One minute Cabir would text a 'Hey'. Keira would reply by asking about his day. He would tell her both the good and the bad. She would lift his spirits with humour followed by laughing emojis. When she had much to say she would call. Sometimes he would come down to her hostel and honk to call her down. She would rush downstairs and spend the next few hours sitting on the bench with him; at times, they would go for a short drive around the city.

When their busy schedules permitted, they would synchronize their library time so they could be together while they worked.

'Why don't you join us?' Cabir made a vague offer as they searched for reference material from the stacks at the Bodleian.

'Why would I join you guys? I don't do rude. Neither am I mean to others nor am I rich and spoilt.'

'So you think I am all of this,' he teased as he pulled her close.

'No,' she shied away.

'Let's just clear this out, enough with your flirting,' he said tugging her hair. 'Tell me what you think of me,' he asked making her blush. (What is a crush good for if seeing him can't make you blush)

'I…I…' she stammered, 'will tell you soon.' She was overwhelmed. It was the first time she had this strong a feeling of blood gushing through her veins.

'Is that our thing?' he flirted, 'I ask you something and you roll your eyes.'

'We do have a thing Cabir. You can't deny that,' she too had learned to flirt back.

'Feels strange right? Going home,' said Sasha as she packed a piece of clothing into her suitcase. She was finishing her packing getting ready to fly back to India the next day when the semester ended and all would head back home for winter break.

'I am not going **home**, not really,' replied Keira who not keen on packing, was occupied in staring at the mirror putting on her lip-gloss.

It was not that she would miss Oxford or even Cabir to such an extent that she didn't want to go away for a mere two weeks; if anything she was terrified.

Terrified of what would be the fate of the 'Malhotra Mansion'. It had been quite some time since the two brothers, her dad and the person she wasn't supposed to call uncle, had been fighting for their share in the family property once grandma left for heaven without a will. What had fate decided for the place she was most attached to? Would it be divided into two halves, rebuilt or left stranded at the hands of some builder, to be turned into a multiplex or a resort? She wasn't eager to find out.

Keira could put the garb of an escapist while she was here at Oxford. She could ignore all the fights, quarrels, jealousy, taunts and tears. But, now she had no choice. She would be forced to confront everything face to face. She was certain that this time it was going to be worse than the last time she had visited the house and was made aware of the horrible possibilities, which stood at the threshold of Malhotra Mansion. It would keep on becoming worse because here's the thing about hate, and also ironically about love: it keeps on growing stronger, entrenching itself deeper and deeper with time.

Her house, her home wouldn't be all decorated in golden and red for the New Year for its inhabitants would instead be busy grabbing each other's necks. The atmosphere wouldn't be filled with the sound of carols but screaming voices accusing each other of deceit and cunningness. The air wouldn't carry the sweet aroma of apple pie but that of pride and prejudice preceding doom. She was neither ready nor willing to witness any of it once she reached **home**.

'Why do you say that?' Sasha asked.

'Uh…Nothing…Just like that…' she said as she tried to escape, yet again. What could she tell her, when she herself wasn't sure of how she felt or how she would react to any of it?

Her phone chimed preventing her from being engulfed by the depressing thoughts of Malhotra Mansion.

'Cabir's here, let's go.' Keira headed towards the door at once. Cabir had arrived downstairs to drive them to a restaurant in London for a final dinner together before everyone left the following day.

'Where are the others?' questioned Sasha, as she intentionally sat in the back seat of Cabir's car with Sid, who too had done the same to let Keira sit next to Cabir.

'They're picking Steve up; they'll meet us at…' He stopped abruptly, 'what happened to you?' He turned to Keira, 'Why do you look like someone just killed a baby bunny?'

'It's just that I don't want to go home,' she groaned. He began driving.

'Me neither. The closest thing I've had to a home is the penthouse at *Four Seasons,*' he empathized. And unlike other people, he could because they knew each other's stories like no one else did. He himself had suffered at the hands of a lunatic family and having heard the story of the Malhotra Mansion from Keira one day when she was utterly cranky, he understood her anxiety.

'What time is your flight?' he inquired.

'It's at 12 noon, British Airways,' she intoned.

'Cancel it,' he said as if his word was final, 'or I will do it for you.'

'What!'

'Don't do something you don't want to.'

'But I have to.'

'No, there is nothing that you have to do, there's always a choice,' he said firmly, 'I will cancel it for you.'

'No, you won't,' she said exasperated; as he continued shaking his head in refusal, 'Cabir!' she yelled.

'What's the matter with you two?' demanded Sasha, who had been busy conversing with Sid.

'Your friend here, doesn't wish to go holidaying with me,' Cabir teased.

'When did that happen?' Keira protested in shock.

'All right then, be ready with your bags tomorrow morning , I'll pick you up at nine,' he ordered Keira who rolled her eyes in annoyance, 'Sid will be visiting his brother posted in Louisiana,' he continued with the discussion of a never-mentioned trip, 'Sasha, would you like to come?'

'I'd love too, but my ticket is non-refundable, so my plan is fixed,' she turned down politely.

'It's decided then,' he said, 'me and Miss Malhotra will have the time of our lives,' he smirked.

'Cabir!' shrieked Keira.

The world can change in a millisecond. People's lives, relations, circumstances, beliefs and deeds can all change in that millisecond. However, the most bewildering thing about that millisecond which is capable of changing our world is that we do not know when it will be, if it will be.

It was their last dinner together in a restaurant located at the bank of Thames, quite close to the Tower Bridge. Filled up with families and couples enjoying pre-Christmas festivities, it was felicitous for celebrations.

All but the two – Cabir and Keira – seemed to be engrossed in the richness of a glass of good wine and the delicious food platters. The latter was pondering upon her broken family and a probable broken house while the former appeared to be occupied with an altogether different math of his own.

'Why are you so restless?' demanded Keira as she held Cabir's leg, which repeatedly tapped the floor.

'All right,' he took an audible breath, 'it is time. Keira can I see you outside,' he requested as he got up. 'Please follow me.'

'Cabir what happened, you are freaking me out,' she said standing up in response to this sudden call for a private meeting. When he didn't respond she turned to the others to apologize for his behaviour. 'Please excuse us for a moment,' she said before following him suspiciously.

'Everything ok with you?' she gathered courage and boldly asked when he finally stopped next to a tree decorated beautifully with Christmas lightings to suit the season. 'Why are you so nervous?'

'Do I seem to be?' he asked feebly. Then looking extremely serious he started in a deeper voice, 'Keira Malhotra…' His voice became intense as he came nearer while she watched in confusion.

'You must know by now that you can make me go weak in my knees, so I better get down on them,' he said and went on his knees. By now, Keira was getting an idea of what he planned to do but she was too overawed and dazed to say or do anything.

He mumbled under his breath, 'I never knew it would be this hard.' He then went ahead and took both her hands in his to gain composure.

'Keira, I haven't done this for anyone before, so please ignore if I goof up,' he smiled looking into her eyes. 'I didn't plan upon this but I had to do this today because on Christmas we tell the truth and I couldn't go for vacations nor could I enter a new year without letting you know this. Keira you're the only one whose thoughts I value more than mine, the only one who yells at me, can actually manage to calm me down,' he expressed emotionally. Something just changes whenever I see you walking towards me, I feel like being good, being myself – just Cabir. I love it when you take my name, I love it when I irritate you and I really love being around you all the time and I think…' he bent his head to kiss her hands as if they were the only thing keeping him rooted to the ground, 'I love you. I love you Keira Malhotra.'

Where words failed, actions succeeded. Keira bent down and raised him up. She pushed him against the tree and running her hands through his hair, she drew him nearer, so close that she could feel his breath and hear his heartbeat before she pressed her lips against his, melting into the slightest yet passionate whisper of a kiss.

Keira turned around to hide the darkest blush spreading across her face after her perfect first kiss. She tried to step away when Cabir pulled her close again. 'Remember what you told me about the stars? How they create a map we have to fill up with beautiful things,' he asked softly as his voice then filled with commitment, 'I promise I'll fill it with the best of moments and memories, just be with me,' he said genuinely.

'I already am.'

'What took you guys so long?' asked Sasha as they sat in their seats. 'C'mon, the food is getting cold.'

'All ok Cabir?' inquired Veronica.

'Yeah, absolutely, everything is great,' Cabir smiled at Veronica and then directed his smile to Keira who nodded in agreement followed by a shy smile.

As they enjoyed dinner that exceptional evening, Keira forgot all about the next day. She did not think of the house, which was miles away from her; all she thought about was Cabir, who was right next to her.

And then, just when she had managed to escape reality without forcefully running from it, it came calling back.

'Why is she calling me?' She appeared frightened as she looked at her ringing phone, 'I mean she rarely calls,' she told Cabir as she got up.

'Hey, do you want me to come outside?' he offered.

'No, it's all right. I'll be right back,' she said trying to sound normal even though at that moment her heart raced as the various prospects of an unexpected call crossed it.

'Hello! Mom!' she answered the phone as she headed outside.

★★★

Let Us Go

'What is taking her so long?' wondered Cabir restlessly after Keira was gone for a few minutes now, 'I'll go check on her,' he pronounced and left the table to go look for her.

'Hey…Hey…' Cabir freaked out as he found her sitting right beneath the very tree from earlier that night while it was still cheerful and faultless and now there she was, sitting on the bare ground with her legs crossed, her head between her folded arms, her hair messed up, sobbing her heart out.

'Keira, your mom, what did she say?' Cabir asked anxiously as he sat in front of her and pulled her head up.

'What will I do?' she whimpered as he wrapped his arms around her and she still in shock just leaned in.

'What do you mean?'

'They sold the Malhotra Mansion, they sold my house, my only home,' she wept harder, '...they just gave it away. Didn't even give me a chance to say goodbye. They sold it!' she moaned. 'Cabir, they're going to demolish my home and build some apartments over it,' she was out of breath, 'and there's nothing I can do to stop it.'

'But why?' Cabir felt helpless. He was unable to console the little child who seemed to have died along with the pronounced death of her house.

'They think that dividing the house would mess things up. Start new fights. So they felt it was better to get rid of it, divide the money and move into separate places,' she lamented as he stroked her hair. 'My parents, they've bought this new flat with their share. Mom just texted me the address,' she added as she attempted to straighten herself up with his help.

'And you know the way she told me about it, is a cliché irony,' she said imitating her mom, 'Keira, we're moving out of that cursed house, into a new flat we just bought, exciting isn't it; **exciting**,' she rolled her wet eyes. 'I'd rather sleep here on the ground than in that stupid flat,' she added heatedly. 'The problem with my family is that they can never see me happy. I was so happy tonight and look what they've turned my happiness into…' She was about to start weeping again when Cabir pulled her up along with him and holding her firmly by the shoulders looked directly at her.

'Listen to me; you cannot believe that,' he said, 'your family they care about you enough to at least update you on their whereabouts. My family – I don't even know which continent my dad is on or on whose bed my mom is sleeping in and they don't know where to find me,' he brought up his own misery to make hers seem a little less adverse, 'Keira we're all messed up, you less than most.'

'Keira? Cabir?' Steve came calling, followed by the others as they reached the nearby parking lot.

'We're here,' replied Cabir as he took his hands off her and headed a few steps in their direction.

'Hey Keira,' called Sasha, 'I want to buy those caramel muffins my mom likes from that bakery we once went to. I'll be going with Steve and Veronica, so it is just you and Cabir.' She winked at Cabir from a distance as they sat in their respective cars and drove away.

'You want to stay here for a little while?' he asked her as she stood still lost in thought.

'No, I want to go back and sleep it off,' she said weakly as they walked towards Cabir's car without further dialogue.

She didn't speak a word on the journey back; she looked lost and tired as she stared out of the rolled down window. All Cabir could do was hold her hand tight the whole way as he drove with just one hand. He didn't pester her to speak. She was heartbroken and not without reason. Her whole foundation had been shattered.

'Hurry up Keira!' Cabir shouted as he got out of his vintage car outside the girls hostel the next morning.

Thinking he was there just to say goodbye before she unwillingly left for her journey home, she headed down to see him. Even though it was already half past nine, and Sasha had already left, lost in thoughts Keira had neither slept nor packed nor was she dressed when she was met by an astonished Cabir.

'Why aren't you ready yet?' he questioned straightaway as she appeared in front of him in her pyjamas.

'What is this for?' she dodged his query and pointed to the luxury vehicle instead.

'This is our ride,' he announced proudly, 'you see I either travel like royalty or I stay at home.'

'So you are here to drop me?' she asked impressed.

'Drop you? Where?'

'At the airport.'

'Why would I drop you at the airport when I myself

cancelled your ticket?' he said confused.

'What!' she yelled, 'You cancelled my ticket. Why?'

'You only agreed to it last night,' he reminded, '...and after all the family drama I thought you'd be more than willing to come with me…'

'Come where?' she said waspishly.

'On a vacation …you knew that right?'

'No I didn't!'

'Well, so I am telling you now,' he said unruffled to a furious Keira, 'We're going on this trip I have planned for both of us.'

'I am kind of homeless right now and you here want to go on a vacation.'

'That is the whole point of it,' he debated his idea, 'You won't have to go home…This will cheer you up. Now go, hurry up and get dressed.'

'I am not going anywhere,' she challenged and turned away agitatedly, but Cabir grabbed her arm immediately and turned her back.

'Look at me,' he said seriously, 'Do you really want to face it? Are you ready enough?'

'No, all right. I am not ready,' she admitted, 'I am just not ready.'

'Then, don't go.'

'But what will I tell them?'

'Make an excuse. Tell them you got caught up with

some work, he suggested, 'or just tell them about the trip, anything you're comfortable with,' he said calmly. 'You can go back there when you are ready, buy yourself some time, clear your head out. Let's keep it that way for now. All right?'

'All right,' she agreed, his crazy idea making sense to her freaked out mind. 'But where will we go?'

'Oh…many places,' he bragged, 'all you have to do is trust me, and ride along.'

'I do trust you Cabir,' she assured solemnly. Then having made up her mind to pause and for once let go of everything but the man who was here for her, she smiled widely and playfully demanded, 'I'll drive.'

'That's my girl,' he patted her back, 'Now you go get ready while I gather the luggage I suspect we still have to pack,' he smiled as they walked up to her room in the half-empty hostel.

'You're taking me to an amusement park? Seriously?' she laughed as she saw humungous rides and playful scenes as their car neared a semi-deserted park in Scotland.

'The little child within you needs to be amused, so this amusement park,' he remarked as they headed to the parking lot. 'I sneaked out of my boarding school once,' he recalled wistfully.

'Why!'

'It was the last day of my sixth grade before I had to go back to that lonely penthouse of mine for the entire summer break,' he described. 'The driver had come to pick me up, but I didn't want to go. So while he grabbed my luggage, I grabbed one of the bicycles and sneaked out.'

'Where did you go?'

'Here of course. This park was my favourite hideout as a kid. I know every nook and corner of this place,' he boasted as they headed towards the park entrance.

'We'll see,' challenged Keira, 'come let's buy the tickets.'

'We don't need tickets,' he said, 'My dad owns this park.'

'Your dad builds skyscrapers, right? Why would he buy a children's park?'

'Believe it or not, he did care for me back in the days,' he sighed. 'When he found out that I liked spending time here he invested in it, merely to ensure the safety of possibly his only child,' he explained. 'He had all the staff look out for me. I have to say, it was infuriating,' he chuckled as they both entered and went on to enjoy an array of different rides until...

'Cabir, look there's a roller coaster!' jumped Keira, 'come let's go,' she pulled him.

'That, Keira is the last ride on earth I would like to be on,' he pulled back, 'and I have no intention of going on it, I just don't like these.'

'Aw...Cabir Dhawan fears a roller coaster,' she poked fun as he shook his head in denial, 'How cute!'

'Keira...'

'How will you scale heights Mr Dhawan, if you are afraid of them?'

'No, it is not like that,' he made a childish *'please let me go'* face.

'Then what is it? You can always tell me.'

'I used to love this thing,' he looked towards the gigantic ride as he reminisced, 'I came here one day when I was ten, instead of going to some benefit dinner my mom wanted me to show up at. She was furious and around eight that night she showed up herself. I was in the front seat of the rollercoaster, had reached the topmost curve,' he pointed towards the highest point of the loop, 'when my mom ordered the operator to shut the ride down.'

'Then?'

'I was left there till the park closed down at eleven,' he said plainly. 'I didn't know what had happened; there were no people around, no one I could call. I screamed and cried. My eyes were all swollen up when they finally let me down,' he exhaled. 'I was so mad I hit the operator, he didn't beat me back of course,' he narrated. 'That was the first fight I got into. Haven't been on any of these since then.'

'Cabir nothing will happen today, besides, your mom is not even here, I am,' she said reassuring him. 'You used to like this ride once.'

'But I don't like it now. So it doesn't matter,' he continued to protest.

'Some things could matter again. You'll like it now, believe me,' she said convincingly.

'If you say so.' He agreed to give it a chance for her sake yet couldn't help adding, 'but if we get stuck up there, I'm going to kill you.'

'Fine, we'll take a knife along, now come,' she implored as she directed him towards the roller coaster.

Cabir grabbed Keira's hand as the ride gained pace, tightening his grip as it went higher and faster. After some seconds, he seemed to be enjoying the ups and the downs, the upside down rolls…when suddenly the ride stopped mid-air, much to Cabir's fear and Keira's chagrin.

'Well done,' he applauded sarcastically, 'We are stuck in here, God knows for how long!'

'It must be some electric failure, it won't be long,' she assured, 'before you are back on the ground.'

'Was it part of your plans today – driving me nuts?' he asked agitatedly.

'Pretty much,' she smiled.

'Keep smiling, I know you find it funny.'

'It is funny,' she laughed, as Cabir grew more restless. 'But it is also beautiful. Just look around you,' she said. The green countryside across which they would be driving soon looked amazing. Picket fences, houses with sloping roofs and red chimneys letting out smoke as a mother inside perhaps cooked lunch; stacks of hay, scarecrows made by the children – all of which appeared tiny to their eyes from the height at which they were caught.

'I've had enough of that beauty,' he said in no mood to look at the world below. He bent down to take refuge in her lap instead.

They were quiet for a while – Keira finding solace in nature and Cabir in her lap, when he spoke again, 'It would have been so much better if you had been here with me on that day when I was stuck,' he said softly.

'I'm here with you now,' she smiled comfortingly.

'You know what, you do drive me nuts when I'm around you,' he complained earnestly, 'But not being around you, also sure as hell drives me crazy.'

They talked for some time as they waited for the ride to restart. Time passed and Cabir dozed off. Charmed by the surroundings and her sleeping boyfriend Keira had no idea how much time had gone by when they finally came down.

They started off late the next morning after checking out of the theme park resort before heading towards the next destination that Cabir still had not disclosed to her as they drove past the stunning countryside of Great Britain on a cloudy afternoon.

'Can you please just tell me where we are going,' she demanded as Cabir directed her to take a left turn at the junction.

'That is the kick Miss Malhotra, not knowing where the road is taking you and yet going wherever it takes you,' he defended as she smiled rolling her eyes at the same time.

As the destination, which Cabir had in mind neared, he asked her to stop the car, switched seats and took the steering wheel. He then took out a blindfold from his dashboard.

'Here, put it on,' he said handing it over to her as he pressed the ignition.

'What? What kind of a kick is this now?' she said but put it on sportingly.

'I am well aware of how crafty you are, and how you will figure out where we are going from the signboards and spoil my surprise,' he clarified. 'You can't now. It's a matter of a mere ten minutes, so wait and watch, oh sorry you can't,' he teased. Now blindfolded, Keira could picture him smirking. She moved her hand to hit her mischievous boyfriend who quickly grabbed and kissed it instead as he began to drive.

'C'mon, slowly,' guided Cabir as he held her from behind while they trekked an uneven land.

'That's enough Cabir, let me take this off,' begged Keira as she walked, still blindfolded.

'We are almost there, just keep going,' he directed as they continued to walk further. It was quiet all around, Keira could hear no human voice except Cabir's; in the silence she could hear the birds and insects chirping, she could feel the cool air touching her face and the tall grass below tickling her legs when Cabir finally helped her remove the blindfold.

'Oh my god!' she bellowed as she opened her eyes to witness the instantly recognizable Victorian railway viaduct surrounded by densely covered mountains, 'I know this place, it's the way to Hogwarts!'

'It is called the *Glenfinnan Viaduct*. This is the route where Harry leaves behind his old life and travels to Hogwarts,' he explained thoughtfully, 'I've got you here so that you too can symbolically let go of whatever you don't want and start afresh.'

They sat there for a while quietly revelling in the serenity of the place. Then they headed to other locations under the

Harry Potter tour of Scotland in Lochaber including the natural lochs of *Eilt, Shiel and Morar* – each having its own unique magical significance. In the evening, they drove to the capital city of Edinburgh ecstatic and content.

'Your key Miss Malhotra,' said the receptionist as Keira and Cabir were done with the formalities before checking into the five starred *Balmoral Hotel* in Edinburgh around 9 pm that night.

'You booked it in my name?' Keira was appreciating his thoughtful gesture when Cabir's attention was suddenly caught by a middle-aged woman, wearing a tight revealing dress and a slightly older man wearing a suit standing beside her.

'What a surprise!' she said walking towards them. 'Cabir darling, what are you doing here?' she asked in a surprised tone moving for a hug but Cabir backed off.

'Zara,' Cabir said with a hint of disgust, 'Dad is not here so don't pretend like you care.'

Keira recognized the women to be Cabir's mother, the London socialite Zara (ex) Dhawan.

'This is Mr Clark, my fiancé,' she introduced the man standing beside her. Cabir made no effort to greet him. 'He owns a fine chain of casinos across the UK,' she boasted, 'and you my darling are?' she turned to Keira.

'Never mind,' Cabir interrupted before Keira could respond, 'You go to the room, I'll join you in a bit,' he requested politely. Keira nodded her head and walked towards the lift.

'I didn't expect to see you here, and who is she?' she questioned when the two of them were left standing alone, once the old fiancé was asked to leave.

'Like I would have still come if I had known that you knew! he scoffed as the two walked towards the lift. 'I never have any idea about where you are, I open Page 3 if I ever want to find out.'

'Have you got those cheques signed from your dad which I had asked you to?' she inquired without taking any offence.

'Now that you people are divorced, this give and take of ours, it's over. I'm sure I made it clear the last time,' he sneered.

'Cabir, don't be silly, I have a deadline for paying Mr Clark.'

'Right. How many shares of his chain is he selling you for the quality time you're going to give him tonight?'

'Cabir, watch your tongue. I am your mother,' she said sternly.

'I guess I should rather watch my feet and get going,' he said as the lift appeared. 'Enjoy your quality time,' he taunted as he stepped in, leaving behind a manipulative and selfish human who had corrupted the purest relation of all – that of a mother and son.

'All ok?' asked Keira as he entered the room and looked around to admire it.

'Absolutely,' he smiled.

'Cabir I can't believe that we are staying in the same room where Rowling stayed; look here,' she enthusiastically pointed towards the writing desk placed near the window, 'This is the very place where Rowling completed the Deathly Hallows,' she referred to the last book of the Potter series. 'I love this place Cabir, thank you.'

'You're welcome' he smiled even as he tried to gain composure after the sudden encounter with the former Mrs Dhawan. He didn't have to pretend in front of her. She knew what he must have felt. She could see the pain behind his smile.

'In 1998, it was J K Rowling who stayed here, in 2018 it was Cabir Dhawan,' she remarked as she came closer, 'both of whom are successful names in the writing business,' she prophesied as she leaned over and gave him a hug.

'Your mom, what did she say?' she asked after a while.

'Nothing, the usual stuff,' he seemed reluctant to discuss the meeting.

'Did you know she was coming here?'

'No, I didn't.'

'Did she know that you were going to be here?'

'No, she did not,' he said firmly, 'in our family we don't know what is going on in the other person's life and we don't care,' he said in a high pitch.

'But she is your mother!' Keira couldn't absorb this hatred between a mother and her only son.

'Then why do I not call her mom!' he yelled as he walked towards the door. 'I need some fresh air.' He banged the suite door and left.

Drained from the day's travelling and unwilling to order food without Cabir, Keira slept early. It was around 12 am when she felt a kiss on her head indicating Cabir's return.

'Cabir…' Keira shook his arm around 3 o'clock that night as he slept on the other side of the bed, 'Wake up sleepy head.'

'What?' he yelped still half sleep.

'I'm hungry.'

'Then order something from room service,' he muttered and switched side.

'No…I want to go out and grab something to eat,' she pestered. 'Cabir!' she nudged him as he was about to fall asleep again.

'Are you insane?' he looked dazed as he checked the time on his watch. 'Where will you find a decent restaurant at three in the morning?' he pointedly asked, sitting up leaning against the headboard.

'We'll see. Just get up and get into the car,' she pleaded as he seemed to consider.

'All right...Get the wallet.' He got down from the bed, stretched his muscles and they stepped out into the deserted corridor.

'What?' he asked annoyed as Keira kept on smiling stupidly while he locked their door.

'Nothing,' she grinned again at the absurdity that she finally had someone whom she could irritate without them leaving her and running away.

'You should be glad that you have an adorable smile, cause this late night madness of yours is super annoying,' he grinned and started childishly running along the long corridor leaving behind both Keira and the sleep that had deserted him now.

'You think you're the only one with the erratic tendency to be weird,' he yelled running faster with a sudden surge of zeal as Keira ran behind him. They raced through the hotel like kids chasing an ice cream truck.

They drove around the town searching the streets before Keira finally spotted a few cars and neon lights glowing and asked Cabir to pull over. It was an old Scottish jazz bar, which was still serving. They walked into a room filled with partially passed-out people slumped on high stools in front of the bar. On the side opposite to the bar was a raised platform on which a live orchestra of aged musicians played soothing jazz melodies. Next to it was an open space dimly lit with red and golden lights where a gay couple danced slowly to the retro harmonies.

'Would you like to dance,' Cabir offered his hand as they finished their snacks and Keira had emptied the glass of bourbon, she'd bugged Cabir to get her.

'I didn't know you could dance,' she commented as they headed towards the now empty dance floor.

'I just feel like sharing my talent with the world today,' he smirked as he held her close and they began to groove slowly, getting lost in the music as they danced.

They came out of the bar an hour later, still grooving to the rhythm that faded into the background. Keira tightly held on to Cabir's arm giggling and tumbling as they made their way to the car.

'Cabir, look there's a cop over there,' she said noticing a cop following them as they exited the bar.

'Damn it!' cursed Cabir as he saw the cop too and whispered to Keira, 'Get ready…on the count of three.'

'One…Two…Three…' he counted and ran towards the car while Keira comprehending his instruction varyingly stood there calling out to the cop.

'Hello? Mr Cop?' she was foolishly calling by the time Cabir, who had run half way to the vehicle realised that his co-partner in the run was missing.

'My God Keira…Run…' he retreated hurriedly to grab her wrist and they began to run. The cop now assuredly suspicious joined the race and began chasing them.

'In, quick,' he directed rushing into the car and in no time raced away from the cop who stood there panting and probably swearing as the two escaped.

'Whoa…That was close,' exhaled Cabir as he slowed down the speeding vehicle once they were back on the highway and far away from the reach of the cop who they splendidly outran. 'Thank God Zara won't have to make an early dawn visit to the station to bail us out,' he laughed.

'But why on earth did we run like muggers. We didn't do anything wrong,' she exclaimed once she caught her breath after a near arrest in a foreign land.

'Oh right. You were going to explain it to the police officer; 'Hey Mr Cop…' Cabir mocked her momentary delusion in an imperfect world.

'How were you going to make him believe that I, coming out of a bar at this late hour wasn't drinking and driving, and you laughing your head out, weren't stoned?'

'I did not think it through,' she admitted and joined him in the laughter.

'That's the thing Keira,' he said in a flirty tone, 'Beauty alone is not enough, you got to use that brain more often.' He ogled at her comically and Keira did her signature eye roll.

'What is it?' he asked after a while as they drove back to their hotel. She seemed lost in thought, as if reflecting upon something while she gazed at the stars above from the open car.

'Cabir, I was wondering,' she said tenderly, 'What if you had not followed me to the bus that day at Heathrow? We wouldn't have been this way.'

'Well…' he took a moment to reflect, 'If not at the airport that day, I would have noticed you another day – chanting prayers walking past the cathedral or sipping an espresso in one of the city cafes or reading a book in the central library. Somehow or the other,' Keira could feel his eyes on her as he answered, 'I would have found you.'

'Rise and shine,' he woke her up drawing the bedside curtains and allowing the bright sunshine to enter the room.

'Let me sleep,' groaned Keira as she pulled the quilt over her face.

'Breakfast is ready,' he tried again.

'10 am…seriously?' she checked his wrist watch, 'I sleep past noon during vacations.'

'Look, get up. We still have so much to cover,' he showed her his itinerary of places to be covered in and around Edinburgh.

'I see…' she raised her head pretending to look at it for a moment only to grab it and crush it the next minute, 'Now we don't,' she giggled when Cabir left for the living room pulling the typical '*Angry Cabir*' face .

'Wait…I'm sorry,' she fell for his fake anger. She sprang out of the bed and at once rushed to the sofa where he sat pretending to sulk.

'It's nice I always keep a copy handy,' he said pulling her hand, shoving her down onto the sofa, 'Caught you,' he growled, whispering into her ear, 'I love you Keira. Now let's order breakfast.'

'What! You said it had already arrived,' she pulled his cheek for his morning pranks before saying it finally, 'I love you too, Cabir Dhawan.'

★★★

Time Out

'What next?' inquired Keira as they checked out of the hotel the next day once they were done exploring Edinburgh. 'I mean I don't want to go home just yet.'

'In that case we don't go home, we go somewhere else,' he proposed with a chuckle, 'Where would you like to go Rome? Paris? Amsterdam?'

'Anywhere will do,' she said amused, 'but for now I guess I should head back to the hostel. Only a few days are left, it won't be too boring.

'Oh sure,' he said sarcastically, 'You have a visa to travel all of Europe, ample free time and a handsome guy devoted solely to your entertainment. Staying in the hostel won't be that boring.'

'All right, where will you take me?'

'To my apartment in London. It is quite an attraction for the tourist Madame,' he smiled, 'We'll halt there for a day or two and then we'll see.'

'I can't wait.' It was a sweet gesture taking someone to your house. He knew how to make her feel special.

They reached London by afternoon, spent the evening in the Warner Bros. Studio and caught a theatre show at the Piccadilly Circus Square.

'Cabir, this place! It's wonderful!' exclaimed Keira when he finally took her to his apartment and showed her around. 'Did you design it?'

'Yes. After Zara moved out and dad transferred the lease to my name, I thought I'll make it my crash pad.' They moved from room to room in the beautifully designed four-bedroom apartment.

Cabir took her to the bedroom. It was dark and silver stars painted with shimmer glowed on the roof. When Cabir switched on the light, Keira noticed the room to be way too clean for a bachelor like him.

'How often do you come here?' she questioned as she glanced at the study with rows of books lined neatly in shelves and a desk filed with files and diaries.

'Not very often, don't feel like coming. The maid comes to clean once a week.'

'Why not?'

'Many reasons, but mainly coz the silence at night tends to deafen me, so I prefer places with people around. You are the first person I have brought here.'

'And I want you to know that it means so much to me,' she smiled.

'You did this!' she jumped in awe as she laid eyes on a world map painted on the entire wall opposite the door with countries and capitals marked. Stuck on it at their respective locations were Polaroids depicting different cities.

'I had help,' he said modestly as they walked out of the room, 'Now, what will you have? Let's order something.'

'No, I want to cook something, let me check what we have in here,' she went on to check the drawers and the refrigerator in his kitchen and found a pack of pasta. 'Pasta?'

'Pasta will be perfect,' he blushed. 'Come let's find the other ingredients, I have no idea what is kept where,' he smiled bashfully as they looked for them.

'Now how about you cook while I attend to some unfinished business nearby?' he said heading out . 'I'll be back home by dinner time, honey,' he called out teasingly as he left.

'Whatever!' Keira began to cook.

'Keira?' Cabir called out warily when he returned half an hour later and found the house filled with smoke. 'Keira, come out!' he yelled in panic thinking it to be some kind of gas leak when Keira appeared through the smoke.

'Don't get mad, if I say that I burnt our dinner. I got too lost looking around,' she made a puppy face.

'You get to the balcony, I'll open the doors and windows,' he acted promptly.

'What will we do now?' Keira asked once in the balcony with him.

'We wait for the smoke to clear out and then we try again. This time I'll help you,' he said confidently.

'You? What do you know about cooking?' she laughed.

'Oh you don't know me; I am a very talented person.'

'We'll see,' she challenged.

They cooked a simple pasta with red sauce accompanied by Cabir's display of MasterChef tricks and a big mess on the slab. The Italian dinner may have lacked salt but what it didn't lack was love.

'Cabir…?' murmured Keira in her sleep as Cabir carried her to the lift in the middle of the night.

Keira was fast asleep when a sudden rocking sensation woke her up.

'Oh my God!' She sat up with a start. Terrified she looked around to find herself lying in the backseat of Cabir's car while he himself sat staring at her from the front seat. The car wasn't moving and yet she could feel it shaking rhythmically. The windows were rolled down and her hair was flying all across her face.

'Good morning,' Cabir smiled as she gathered her hair and straightened up.

'What the hell Cabir!' she said annoyed, 'where are we? and why on earth is this car shaking?' she rattled questions one after the other.

'Because…we are on water.'

'What! We're on a boat!' she exclaimed as she attempted to open the car door immediately.

'**Yacht**,' he corrected as she got down to stand utterly stunned on the deck of a yacht as it sailed smoothly across the ocean cutting through the winds of the European North Sea.

'So you actually did carry me down. I wasn't dreaming!'

'God! It was so peaceful when you were sleeping,' he said coolly as she swivelled around seeing nothing but the blue sea, a car parked on a yacht and Cabir Dhawan who smiled at her casually as she went on a full-blown panic mode.'

'I mean I sleep at night on a bed and wake up on a

yacht – genius. Where did you get this thing from?'

'It's Dad's. I borrowed it for us.'

'What was so important that it couldn't wait until morning?' she demanded, 'where are we?'

'In Monte Carlo.'

'…Monte…France!' She jumped, 'Are you crazy! I am not going to France.'

'Well technically we are already in France,' he pointed out towards the long island, which became slightly visible as they slowly sailed.

'How could you!' she went on grumpily, 'No one knows where I am; mom and dad think I'm in London, I myself have no idea about what is going on. You should've told me!'

'This is exactly why I didn't tell you,' he said referring to her manic outburst. 'That's the problem with you Keira; you think way too much – planning, analysing; results, consequences – you want it all sorted out, all in your control,' he lashed out. 'And that is not how things happen in life. You can't control everything every time… When life gives you lemons, you squeeze it over some chicken and let it go!'

'But…'

'And you know what makes you even more miserable,' he went on as Keira listened, silenced by his sudden outburst, 'You care too damn much about what other people think. What will happen when you go home? How will your parents react to your little trip? What will Sasha and Steve say about us being together? You have thought about it all, haven't you?' he asked confidently, Keira nodded. He paused to ask, 'Do you trust me?'

'Yes.'

'Then trust me and do yourself a favour – stop pitying yourself; love yourself a little more. Take a timeout, go to a place where you know no one, and no one knows you. Let your mind rest while your heart makes the choices.'

He was telling aloud the very same things she wanted to shout out to herself.

Cabir walked to her with two life jackets as the French shore of the sunny and glamorous islands of Monte Carlo became distinctly visible.

'What's this for?' she asked as they put them on and Cabir walked towards the bow. She followed.

'You feel all right? Do you know how to swim?' he asked.

'Of course.'

'Great. Then be ready to jump,' he announced as they stood at the edge of the yacht.

'What!' Keira shrieked in disbelief but didn't have a chance to debate for the next moment Cabir grabbed her hand and jumped right into the sea, pulling her along as he did.

'Help! Help!' Keira began to shout on top of her lungs as soon as they hit the water. Frightened she sprang up to hold him, her arms tightening around his neck she roared, 'Have you lost your bloody mind! We're going to drown!'

'We won't. That's what these life jackets are for.' He let her hold on to him. 'Now relax, take a deep breath and swim towards the shore.'

She looked at him with faith and followed his directions. She withdrew her hands, took a breath to fill her lungs with all the oxygen required to 'save her life' and began to swim after him steadily with all her strength as he started swimming towards the coast, which was a few meters away.

They swam all the way to the shallow waters of the French coast and then walked towards the beach.

Totally exhausted Keira lay panting on the sand while Cabir stood over her breathing rapidly and simultaneously laughing at her as if they'd just come out of a resort pool.

'Did you enjoy it?' he asked.

'Enjoy it! I could have died!' She too began to find the daftness risk worthy.

'That's a bit melodramatic,' he continued laughing. Keira clutched his arm and pulled him down next to her. He fell on his back and they both lay giggling on the sand; sunbathing without any sunscreen or umbrella in the town conjuring visions of a glamorous bygone era where the coastline was dotted with super yachts and the streets lined up with sophisticated but charming high rise hotels and exotic shops.

'Would you have regrets if you died today?' he asked casually, once they caught their breath.

'Everyone would have regrets. Things they could have said or done,' she replied calmly.

'I don't know why we don't say what we mean to, or just go ahead and do something we have an instinct for. What stops us?'

'The fear of knowing what might happen if we did,' she said thoughtfully, 'We choose to live with the regret of not doing a thing rather than standing up to the fear of doing something that might go wrong,' she sighed, 'Like I always wanted to buy my own house.'

'That's unusual.'

'…But then I fear what if I can't, what if I do and no one comes back to live in it. I rather end up not buying it and then wondering what if I had,'

'It's all about the **what if's**,' he sighed, 'I always wanted to scuba dive. What if I did?'

An idea struck him as he turned to face Keira, '**What if** we find out tomorrow, I know this place nearby where we can go for a dive.'

'You had an instinct, you said it out loud. Now we do

it', she agreed willingly, 'without a **what if**.'

'All right then we jump back into the sea tomorrow,' he said getting up.

'I'll push you first this time,' she promised.

'Now Mr Genius, do you know what we are going to do? We're all wet and covered in sand; we have no phones or cash or cards,' It seemed as if she had quickly learned to laugh at the face of uncertainty life threw at them from time to time.

'Just tag along...' He gave her a hand and the two ambled through the radiant and vibrant beach; letting the sun dry their clothes, the air blow away the sand stuck on their bodies and the land absorb their fears.

'Cabir…!' Keira called out as adrenaline rushed into her veins.

They both sat geared up in their diving equipment ready to dive into the North Sea, three miles away from Monte Carlo. The motor boat had just stopped above their diving spot. They had been practicing in shallow waters for the past two days and now at any moment, they would be instructed to make the final dive into the deep water and witness the glory beneath the ocean.

'Cabir I…' she began to pour out her heart and he understood even before she finished.

'Love you,' he completed, 'I know.'

'Promise me this is forever,' she said as they took positions for the jump.

'I promise,' he ensured. They put the oxygen tube into their mouths, looked at each other and jumped.

'To the mighty ocean,' toasted Cabir as they sat at an outdoor beachside diner late that evening after their dive. They were celebrating their victorious adventure with bottles of beer.

Monte Carlo had been a blessing. In the three days they spent here, they did things they never had before; Cabir did karaoke in one of the rooftop bars, Keira got a portrait of herself done from a roadside artist; they both joined the local street dancers and shook a leg, they felt fully present in their present.

Sitting at the diner amidst holidaying tourists and artists playing French songs on guitars with lyrics only a few could understand but music all could feel, forced them to re-evaluate their own lives, get comfortable with uncomfortable truths and pledge to look at their lives from a new perspective.

'Right now I wouldn't want to be anywhere else or with anyone else but here with you,' she expressed eliciting a tender smile from him.

'You can go anywhere you want with me – Tokyo,

Sydney, New York?' He offered laughing.

'Stop!' She laughed at the absurd possibilities which she would definitely want becoming future realities, 'Tell me why Monte Carlo. Most people who come to France go to Paris first?'

'Coz you and me, we're not most people.'

'But I wanted to see the Eiffel Tower and Disneyland,' she pouted.

'So you want to go to Paris?'

'Yes.'

'You want to go to the city of lights.' he said loudly with bursting fervour.

'Oh Yes…!'

'Louder.'

'Yessss...Yes…yes,' she screamed. A few heads turned to see where the noise came from. They didn't care.

'So, it's decided then, Paris it is!' He shouted back and they cheered – with another round of beers – to the city of life and love.

***

The Last Spring

When the University reopened for the new term, Keira and Cabir returned to Oxford together. All their friends were also back. They decided their friends deserved to know about their relation. They didn't want the ones they cared about coming to know of it in any other way or from someone else and so one by one they disclosed it to each of their friends.

Cabir's friends were astonished that he had let someone in so quickly and easily. Veronica took credit for encouraging him in the first place to open up and get the girl. Sid gave them both relationship advice, proving how it's true that those who have no experience in dating often give the best advice.

Steve who had been constantly on and off with Veronica wasn't elated with the idea of someone else getting into a relationship. Sasha on the other hand was thrilled with the news; she gave them both a hug and announced that she knew something was cooking up between them and that Keira had had a 'thing' for Cabir since the very beginning.

Any student walking past the open parks or corridors of the University of Oxford that spring was likely to notice Keira and Cabir, either sitting together on one of the benches, walking next to each other on the street or meeting in between classes. On weekends, they'd accompany each other to the library, in the afternoon they'd head to a local café and at night Cabir would often park his car at her hostel and ritually honk to call her down.

They spent that spring together – strolling in the Church gardens or sitting under the trees that drew greener and blossomed with flowers as the season peaked. As they sat on the bench, completing their assignments Cabir would look up from his paper and just gaze at Keira. Keira too would do the same, stare at him as he sat engrossed in thoughts as he wrote. Sometimes he would recite his poetry or let Keira read his writings, which she would appreciate and sometimes help improve.

Everyone had a different opinion on their relationship; some would adore them and look up to them as 'couple goals' while others felt differently. Some would wonder how Cabir had finally managed to woo a girl or how Keira had chosen a boy like Cabir over all the other potential aspirants who chased her.

It was all new to Keira but she was happy with all that she had now and didn't really care about any of it. But Cabir – also new to all this – cared way too much about what people said this time. Why wouldn't he? After all, the comments and gossips and the furtive glances involved Keira and not him alone.

Theirs wasn't a fairy tale which ended with everyone happy right after the grand proposal. Just like any other couple, they too had differences, matters to quarrel and fight about but what was unique to them was how each of their little debates would end up with declarations of love.

'Cabir how dare you turn your back to me!' Keira demanded as they collided outside the Great Hall one evening, look at me!'

'And then do what?' he said irked by her tone.

'Tell me what the hell is up with you!'

'Nothing.'

'Cabir!'

'Keira!'

'You got suspended,' she raised her voice '...and how do I get to know, from Veronica and not you, because Mr Dhawan didn't bother informing me?'

'So what?' he argued, 'Yes I got suspended for a week; this isn't the first time.'

'Yes it isn't the first time, but it is the first time since we have been together!'

'**Since we have been together**,' he nodded, 'a lot has changed since then.'

'Love does that Cabir, it changes you.'

'Huh,' he dismissed, 'so why is it that suddenly it has become so important for everyone – you, your friends, even my friends – to keep me in check?'

'Yes it is. Think of it Cabir, every time we quarrel or someone says something about us, you or me or your parents; you go ballistic. Being good doesn't mean being good only to me. So tell me is it so wrong for us to try to keep you in control?'

'Keira, I know you care about me,' he refused to give in, 'But this is how I am, this is how I was before and I'm not going to change.'

'I don't want you to change Cabir. It's just that this destructive behaviour you have adopted, it's bad for you. Period.'

'You know what's bad?' he switched to a more serious tone, 'I'm bad for you Keira. You should be the one turning away from me; that is what you should have done months ago.'

'Yeah right, so that you can go berserk any time you want!'

'It's not about that. You don't understand...' he faltered, 'I can't change myself and I can't afford to change you!'

'You're giving yourself way too much credit!' she shouted.

'Am I? Don't you spend all your day trying to calm me down; I get angry as many times a day as people eat food!' he pointed out, 'I'm sorry.'

'Really? You're sorry?' she said provoked, 'Then I'm sorry too, coz I am not going anywhere. I knew how you were when I chose you, I love you; and that is something that is not going to change,' she shouted and put an end to the argument by giving him a kiss.

'Just so you know,' he said as they walked into the hall to meet their friends, 'I didn't lose my temper today.'

'You'll duly get your golden star my boy,' she mocked, 'now if you'd tell me what happened that you got suspended?'

'As if you don't know already; still you always insist on my version of every incident,' he said. 'When I was leaving after seeing you at the hostel, some boy, I don't know his name, started blabbering about how I was wasting my time and yours in a relationship that wouldn't work, how I wasn't serious about you and should stop fooling around.'

'So you beat him?'

'Yes I did. I heard he fractured his wrist. I already had

been given a warning before this incident; so this time they suspended me.'

'Well, you know you are not fooling around, I know we are not wasting any time. We both know that we will make this work, so that solves it right. Let them say what they want to. Now let us decide what you are going to do with this week which you have managed to free for yourself.' She took the matter calmly and smiled at him as they entered the hall.

Keira sat opposite him engaged in a conversation with Steve as Cabir ate his food watching her intently.

'I like smiling faces,' Sasha who was sitting next to him said.

'Are you talking about Steve?' he inquired.

'I know Steve looks gorgeous when he smiles,' she pretended to swoon a little, 'but no, it is Keira who I'm talking about. I mean just look at her,' she pointed towards Keira who was smiling widely, her eyes shining and her cheeks glowing as she talked. 'Since you'll got back from Paris, something is different about her – she is so happy all the time, smiling and laughing all day long,' she softly expressed her observation. Cabir listened thoughtfully.

'So?'

'What I want to say is that it is because of you Cabir,' she said. 'She has found someone who makes her happy.

This is the way she is when you are around. And look at yourself, you don't look so bad either,' she patted his arm.

'Love is messy, not everyone gets to be with the one they love,' she stole a glance at Steve, then continued, 'Now that you two have each other, don't mess it up, for anyone or anything.'

'Sasha, you still might have a chance with Steve,' he said keeping in mind the growing differences between Steve and Veronica.

He didn't comment on Sasha's appeal to not let go of the love they were lucky enough to find in this whole wide world. He had never been good at expressing his feelings to a third person. He would listen and absorb everything but never discuss. Cabir Dhawan may have been a robust college bully but the matters of his heart, he always held back.

'Maybe, when the time is right,' she sighed, 'but for you two, this is your time. Enjoy it.'

'I guess this bench is on the verge of being named after you,' she said humorously (She adored the way they pulled each other's leg) as she arrived at the very bench where she and Cabir first sat together the night of his parent's divorce and had been sitting on almost every day since the last semester.

'Welcome to my humble abode then,' he returned the humour as she sat at their preferred place.

'I have written something for you,' he took out this huge diary from his satchel and directly opened the page marked with a bookmark where he had written a piece of poetry he had dedicated to Keira.

'For me! Will you read it to me?' she asked joyously. She liked it when he recited his works to her.

'Nah!' He refused and put on his satchel. 'I wouldn't be comfortable, you reading out my very heart as I sit next to you gawking,' he said as he got up, 'Besides I have to return these to the library by this evening,' he made an excuse and with a slight blush colouring his face he left.

Keira moved her hand across the page filled with his handwriting, watched him go out of sight and then began to read:

We met through fate
We had the same taste,
Had made the same mistakes,
And so, I found in you my best mate.

Now, every moment I am with you,
You make me feel special and new.
With you I feel blessed, I really do,
You're the only one I look forward
sitting next to.

You are my shining chivalrous knight,
Protective, for me you'll always fight.
You're the One there for me,
anytime of the night.
You're the One who tells me whether I'm
going wrong or right.

You're the One, who takes me for
mid-night drives,
It's with you I feel most alive
You are the One, who can wipe away
all my tears,
You're the One who conceals my fears.

I'm only consoled by your hugs,
You're the only one with whom I'll
share my hot chocolate mug.
You're the One with whom I wanna
enjoy the rain,
It kills me to see you in the
slightest of pain.

You are the One holding whose hand
I travel,
You're the One I recite to all my
fantasy fables.
You're the One for whom I'll save
my last dance,
You're the One with whom I'll sneak
out, given any chance.

You're my mischief partner,
You're the One with whom the room is
bound to be filled with laughter.
Laying eyes on you, it felt like skipping
a heartbeat,
A tear rolling down your cheek, is my
greatest defeat.

You are the One till eternity I'll trust,
You're the One embedded in my heart
from core to crust.
You are my day's brightest sunshine
My sole lifeline.

You're the One stroking my head in
moments dry,
You're the One on whose shoulder I can
comfortably cry.
You're the One with whom I'm myself
and never shy,
When with you time simply
keeps passing by.

You are the One with whom under the
stars I wanna lie,
For we've got an unbreakable tie.
You're the One with whom I can
freely talk,
You're the One with whom I wanna take
my life's walk.

My love for you is blindfolded,
And I know no matter what, it would
never get moulded.

She was spellbound. His work was simple, sweet and yet so passionate that even after reading it she kept on staring at the open pages lost in the wonder of how someone could mean so much to anyone, how she had come to mean so much to him.

Cabir was not someone who would pour out his heart. His writings would never express the emotions that lay hidden in the depths of his heart. But this, the first thing he had written for Keira, it lay bare his very heart, a heart he had opened to Keira, a heart she was capable of healing. He had let Keira in, and Keira had promised to never walk out.

Keira closed her eyes for a moment and in her mind, for the very first time came the image of him and her, lying on a bed of their house for an afternoon nap after a hearty brunch while their children played in the backyard. A fantasy surfaced to her consciousness where they were together and so in love even after the passage of many years.

Keira flipped through some other pages of his diary, quickly going through some of his other works as she waited for him to return any moment.

She was thinking about how she would express her love for his poem and for him when her eyes fell on a torn yellow envelope slipped between two pages.

She pulled it out and glanced at it. It was addressed

to Cabir's apartment in London. She opened it. Enclosed within was a typed letter. She went on to read it.

> Dear Mr Dhawan,
>
> Subject: Acceptance into the Mass Communication programme of UCLA.
>
> We are pleased to inform you that after going through your application for our three-year postgraduate programme in Mass Communication, we are glad to offer you a place along with an internship of four months upon the completion of your course.
>
> As of now, we are waiting for the final confirmation for the same from your side, latest by the end of this month. An admissions counsellor will soon get in touch with you. For further details on fee structure and course dates please visit the university website.
>
> Congratulations and regards,
>
> Admissions Department
> University of California & Los Angeles, USA

***

Alaahada

Keira had often heard: When in love, your brain stops working and if it doesn't then it isn't love. Today she realised it was true.

She had been so lost in love that the thought of the year-end nearing, bringing her closer to her final year and Cabir towards completing his graduation had skipped or in fact never really crossed her mind.

However, that was reality. The last semester of the year had already begun, the final exams were around the corner and soon Cabir would finish his literature course and after that, life would take a different course, for her in Oxford, for him elsewhere leaving her wondering about their future.

She had never thought what would happen once he was done with college. However, now the question lay bold and magnified in front of her in form of this acceptance letter.

Cabir had not told Keira about the letter or about him applying to a university on another continent and yet it was in the very diary he had handed over to her. Cabir was not stupid; it was either his way of telling her indirectly or perhaps he too was so deep in love that he'd forgotten placing the letter in the diary – Keira didn't know.

She simply slid it back into his diary, closed it and waited for him. When he came back, Keira praised his work and let it go at that. He looked happy; so she didn't bring up the topic of graduation which she now realised was arriving way too soon.

She kept looking at Cabir with awe filling her eyes. He was so familiar that it felt like she was looking at a part of herself. In the year and a half they had spent getting to know each other she had got so used to him that the sudden thought of him not being around or sitting right here with her on this bench was unbearable.

Reading that letter had broken her heart. She didn't want to let him go, not even out of her sight; but she knew that eventually she would have to. She loved him. She couldn't be selfish with him.

In all their time together, Keira had never hesitated in expressing herself to him. She would tell him anything and everything. But this was that one time she didn't know what to say to him or how to console herself.

They had made so many beautiful memories together but those memories would not be enough to last a lifetime, a life they both at some point or the other had considered spending together.

The term end was nearing and the exams had already begun. Graduation buzz was everywhere and avoiding talking about it even now in the hope of preserving what they had until the very last second seemed foolish.

Growing up wasn't something they could run away from. They had to face it together. So even though Cabir had never mentioned his going away or rejecting a place or any of his related plans after graduation which was due next week, Keira made up her mind to get him to give her some answers – answers she was afraid of hearing and at the same time longed for.

It was the day they gave their final paper. Apart from a handful of days leading to the farewell party for the outgoing batch, it was all over. The juniors were distributing tickets for the farewell dance party the following Saturday when Keira entered the Great Hall and mustering all her courage walked towards Cabir who sat there munching snacks.

'Where is everybody?' she inquired as she took a seat next to him.

'Some of them are with Veronica, the rest are with Steve,' he answered. They had this massive fight about Veronica going off to India for some voluntary work after graduation while Steve has to stay here and complete his degree,' he explained. 'I think they might break up.'

His last sentence froze the blood in her veins. Their situation was no less complicated than that of their friends and their friends seemed to have just lost the battle against their changing lives.

'You didn't go to Veronica?' she asked.

He simply shook his head and said nothing more and she knew exactly why – he was worried about the same thing happening to their relationship.

'Can I ask you something?'

'Anything,' he replied with a look on his face that immediately gave her cold feet and she once again lost her nerve to ask what she'd come for.

'Will you take me to your farewell dance?' she asked instead.

'Of course, who else would I take?' he asked surprised that she would ask something that was so obvious.

It was the day of the farewell party that took place

before the formal graduation ceremony. The vacant grounds of Christ Church were decorated with white tents and magenta lights. The DJ started by playing peppy music and then gradually shifted to slow music as the senior year students, dressed in formals for the occasion, entered leading their dates for the evening.

'Looks like I should wear this tailcoat more often,' Cabir commented later as they sat down to drink wine after dancing with some of Cabir's friends from the senior year.

'Why do you say that?' asked Keira.

'Coz your eyes have not left me all evening,' he said. He had felt her eyes on him and him alone throughout the night.

'The floor is open for one last dance,' announced the DJ as he put on a romantic track and couples slowly walked towards the floor which was now lit neon blue.

'Can I have the pleasure of having this last dance with you,' Cabir asked offering his hand. Keira took it and they began to dance. But this dance wasn't like the one they had back in the jazz bar; the steps were heavier and so were the hearts which knew that so much had changed already and more was going to from now on.

Keira could not take it any longer. She could not bear to listen to his heartbeat as he pulled her closer. She could not bear to feel his hands touch her skin or stare into his eyes, which pierced her own eyes that were welling up.

Knowing that after this night things might never be the same, that he may not be here with her tomorrow, she could take it no more.

'Are you going to leave me?' her voice trembled as she asked while they still grooved to the waltz.

'No Keira. I would never do that,' he assured. At this Keira let out a sob and turned away from him.

'Keira, don't do that. Look at me,' he pleaded. 'I know you've read the letter. I know because you have started behaving awkwardly around me since then.' He pulled her back into his arms, '...and I am not going anywhere without you.'

'You should have told me. Why didn't you tell me?' she cried.

'I didn't know what to say to you. I still don't,' he said honestly. 'I am not going to LA so it doesn't matter.'

'It matters and you know it Cabir,' she asserted, 'that is why you sent an application in the first place.'

'It was a long time ago. I hadn't met you then and I wanted to prove to my father that I could do something away from his shadow. But things are different now, I'm different.'

'This can be your chance of doing something that you really want to; to be somebody. Meeting me shouldn't change what you want to do with your life,' she said emotionally. 'I'm not your life Cabir; I am a part of it. Just like that University is another part of it. So you should go. Go!'

'I knew you would say that.' Keira could see tears filling his eyes.

'What else should I say when I know that I'll be holding you back from doing something you love.'

'I love you Keira Malhotra. You should know that.'

'I do…Cabir,' she said choking up, 'Trust me it is for your own good.'

'Good!' he jerked his neck scoffing. 'How can anything in my life be good if you are not a part of it?'

'It is just a matter of three to four years and then you can come back to me and we can be together.'

'And how am I even supposed to survive each day without you?' He became angry. Now don't say in the same way I did before you. Coz I am not willing to go back to a miserable life that doesn't have you in it. I am not going anywhere. I can't. I don't want to spend my days looking at your picture on my cell or playing your memory in my head...I want to be here with you. I want you to be here with me.'

'I am not going anywhere Cabir,' she pointed towards his heart, 'I am going to be in here all the time, with you.'

'Oh, don't give me that crap,' he tried to move his hand away.

'Cabir…stop,' she held on to the hand and kissed it, wetting it with her tears. He wrapped his hands around her tightly again and whispered, 'I am not letting you go,' he made it clear as he stroked her head.

'Cabir…this…it has to end,' she said firmly as she broke away, 'It's too damn hard.'

'No you are right...' he said, his temper flaring, 'It's fine. Anyone I care about leaves me anyway. For three years or for my whole life it doesn't matter because no one ever stays.' A tear rolled down his eye.

It was the first time that Keira saw him cry. She quickly moved her hands to wipe off his tears but he took a step back, wiped them off with his sleeve and walked away from her.

'So I guess I'll see you around sometime,' he shouted back and left without a goodbye. He had never been good at goodbyes.

The waltz was still playing when Keira Malhotra fell apart right at the floor. She could neither raise her voice to call him back nor could she run after him. He had made his choice and so had she. No one dared to go after Cabir though a few friends came over to calm Keira down. But all those people being around didn't matter for the one person she wanted near her was gone.

'Hey,' Cabir greeted Sasha casually the next morning, 'I was looking for you.'

'Cabir what have you done to Keira?' she asked

ignoring his greeting. 'She didn't sleep last night, I could hear her sobbing. She didn't even get out of bed today. She has never missed a class in college,' she went on without pause, 'so whatever it is that went wrong between you and her last night, fix it.'

'Give this to her for me,' he handed over an envelope to her, 'Tell her that I am sorry.'

'Why don't you tell it to her yourself?' she asked, 'Don't go to such extremes. Do the normal thing – go and talk to her.'

'I'm afraid I can't do that. I am flying to California tonight.'

'What! So you won't be staying for graduation?' she asked shocked. He nodded.

'Who will I go to if Steve asks me out anytime soon?' she pleaded trying to convince him.

'Sasha, stay with Keira. She will need you,' he requested, 'I'll see you around sometime soon,' he smiled half-heartedly and then hugged her before leaving.

Sasha went back to the hostel room where Keira still lay hiding under her blanket. She gave her the envelope and left, giving her the space she needed.

Keira immediately sat up straight, rubbed her eyes dry and opened the letter. The moment she opened it her eyes fell directly at the end where the ink was smudged. Tears, which probably had rolled off Cabir's cheeks once he finished writing; now at the same spot Keira's tear drops spilled as she began to read.

Dearest Keira,
You were right. Love does change us. Starting with I never saw myself writing anything near a love letter. But here I am, trying to express myself to you on this blank sheet of paper.
Though I should go about explaining to you my decision, all I can think about is how much I want to grab you and throw you into one of my cars, and take you to a place far away from this chaos—a place where we can be together and happy. I will do exactly that eventually, just not right now.
Coz right now is the time for me to confess that even though we don't want our lives to change the slightest bit, even though I know that I'm going to be miserable every day I am compelled to spend without you, I have decided to go to UCLA.
Yes, Miss Malhotra I'll do the right thing and I'll do what is right by you, do what you would want me to.
It is taking every ounce of my strength to walk away from you, even for these three years, which I fear to us, will seem like

eternity. I know you understand that. In this time, we both will, I'm sure, relive the time we spent getting to know each other and growing in love, every day. We will at times feel incomplete, in need of one another. We will be haunted by the longing for at least a trembling touch.

But Keira, if ever in my time away I happen to hear your voice over the phone, look into your radiant eyes or see you smiling at me via Skype, I will want to come back flying to you and hold you in my arms; and if I hold you once again I will never be able to leave you. I am not that strong Keira; I am just not.

What we share is something I have never felt in my life or will feel ever again. I would give anything to protect what we have. Keira I want to have it all, or not at all...anything in between would only make us weak and I can't bear that.

I am respecting your choice Keira. I hope that you will respect mine.

Keira Malhotra, you are the best influence on me, someone who pulled me out of the gloom that dominated my life. I may have only known you for two years, but these two years have been the best two years of my life. I feel the stars have blessed me by gifting me you; as if paying me back for all the suffering I have endured at their hands.

I feel extremely lucky to be leaving

knowing that I found what people spend most of their life searching for; I leave knowing that I am loved by no ordinary person but you.

Being in love with you has given me passion, it has consumed me, thrilled me and challenged me and I wish for nothing more but for it to last forever.

This separation is just a little price I have to pay in order to reunite with you in such a way that I never have to leave again. It is a chance I have to take to build a life for us. This is not a goodbye. It is just until I come back to you and we have a June wedding (Yes I am proposing).

Keira, take care of yourself. Time won't stand still, neither should you. The world needs you more than you know and so do I. I will not ask you to not miss me, do. But be happy. I will. I promise.

All my love, as always

Cabir

PS – I have enclosed a photocopy of the registration papers of your family property in Chandigarh along with a deed in your name. I put my money to some good use and bought the house from the dealers it was sold to.
Malhotra Mansion is yours now. Your memories are not going to go anywhere and neither am I.

★★★

After 4 years

Ghosts Of The Past

The sky was moonless and dark clouds hid the stars. The night was still and silent except for the twittering of the birds that flew back to their homely nest. Keira Malhotra who had also flown back to her old hometown Chandigarh a week ago, on her last day in the city, hours before she boarded a flight to her current home in London, decided to visit her **'Home'**.

Her chauffeur-driven car stopped at the gate of a house. A single glance at the house was enough for her to conclude that it was abandoned and aging. She got down from the car, took a few reluctant steps towards the gate and moved her hand over the dirt-covered nameplate. As she scraped the dirt off with her bare hands the words inscribed on it became clear once again – MALHOTRA MANSION.

She let out a sigh, opened the gate and entered the house. It was empty. Malhotra Mansion was no longer home to those who had made it a home once upon a time – some of them were now dead, then there were those who were dead to Keira and those to whom perhaps Keira was dead now. Yet it was ironic how the memories of moments lived here with those very people who had left it to wear out and die were the ones that had made it alive.

She took a hesitant step in, and with each following step flashed glimpses of memories, memories buried in her mind, which now popped up in array in front of her overflowing eyes.

She looked around in despair. The grass was no longer green and maintained but wild and dry, the garden flowerless and the driveway without cars. No joyful noises of children running echoed in the compound. No lights lit up as night approached. Even the cacophony of frogs seemed louder than the sounds from the past.

She pushed aside the cobwebs that obstructed her way and walked through the front porch, which had longed to hear her footsteps these past four years. She staggered through each room and turned away as she realized how each brick was so familiar, how to every corner of the house was attached an emotion.

The walls inside were pale and bare of paint in some places, no longer painted shining white for festive seasons ever since its inhabitants had found a new house to call home. The kitchen and the dining hall stood barren deprived of sweet aromas and laughter shared during meals. The rooms lay vacant cleared of furniture, chatter and love. Her own room rid of its posters was now a mere square where the ghosts of her past had gathered to bring back the turmoil she had escaped these four years by choosing not to visit this forsaken edifice she had once called home.

Coming here and confirming with her own eyes that what she still called home wasn't real anymore and existed only as a delusion in her head totally shattered her from the inside and she curled down on her bedroom floor and broke down; crying over something that she knew was lost forever.

She lay there shedding tears over collapsed memories for about an hour after which her driver came in looking for her. He was alarmed seeing her half-unconscious on the dusty floor. Not knowing what to do, he blurted out that it was nearly time for her flight and that they should start heading towards the airport. It took her wretched mind a while to process his words after which she pulled herself together and walked out.

Walking past her beloved mango tree in the backyard

she remembered the time capsule she had buried underneath it fifteen years ago. She had hoped that one day her family and she would sit down together and open it to rediscover treasures from moments snatched away by capricious time. But now that wish hardly seemed possible and resolving to have mercy on herself by not coming back here again, she managed to find a shovel and dug it out herself, using her painful rage as fuel for the labour. She did not have guts to open it straightaway and handed it over to the driver to keep safely with her luggage.

And then just like all the other members of the Malhotra family, she too turned her back on the home which kept calling out to her, asking her to stay. She reached the gate, turned around for a final glance and with an unspoken goodbye; she walked out straight to her car without looking back.

The ghosts, that had haunted Keira for so long were now trapped within a house she owned but couldn't rebuild. Keen to follow her wherever she went, the recurring ghosts of her past kept on banging against the gates as the driver locked the entrance of the Malhotra Mansion.

She looked at the streets of Chandigarh as her car hurriedly drove to the airport. While Chandigarh seemed more or less the same since her last visit, her life had changed drastically.

After graduating from Oxford with a gold medal, she interned with a financial firm which fetched Keira her first permanent job as an economic consultant in 'TraveloGlobe' – a rising English company managing tours and travel arrangements.

Since then she had been working a nine-to-five job, staying until eight on most weekdays. She would spend the weekends at posh London clubs or in malls with friends from work or her usual companions from college – Steve and Sasha. Steve was looking at professional training in football while Sasha, through Keira's recommendation had landed a job in her company. Both Steve and Sasha had grown quite close during the last year of college while Keira tried desperately to combat her loneliness. They had been dating ever since and were now engaged. They planned to marry by the end of the year.

As for Keira, she had been working in the company for three years now during which the company had benefited immensely from her strategies, innovations and presentations. Now the company was one of the top companies in the travel business.

A latest development initiated by Keira had brought a surprising amount of fortune to her company and had been greatly beneficial to her growing career; earning her the respected designation of the company's assistant CEO in a short span of time. She had been on the post for over four months now and had been working harder than ever since.

A recent article in the *Forbes* magazine featuring her name among the top ten potential company CEO's under the age of thirty proved that she had finally arrived. All of this had brought along with it a fair share of recognition and fame in the business sector of London, with the economic media following her every move. However with it came the toll of competition and jealousy, at times even from Sasha whose relation with Keira grew more distant with every cover story.

Keira spent less time in the humble bungalow she had completed constructing last year on the outskirts of London and more time in her luxury cars travelling around to crack deals and to hold or attend meetings. As the fresh face representing her company she quite often had to travel internationally for associate parties, gatherings and promotions which resulted in her spending more time with the airhostesses on her company's private jet than with her remaining friends.

It was one such deal that had brought her to India, when after attending to her work she had sneaked off to Chandigarh.

As she sat in the airport lounge waiting for her plane, she unlocked her phone to put it on the airplane mode for there was no one she was looking forward to speaking to, no one who would call her before she boarded an eight-hour long flight.

She stopped when her attention fell on her screen saver. It was a picture of her with her father, riding horses on the day of the police parade. She was sitting on a brown pony, holding to it tightly while Mr Malhotra wearing his uniform sat confidently on a black beauty.

'Daddy…wait,' she remembered being scared. It was the first time she had ridden a horse. 'Mommy, I'm going to fall.' She recalled the exact moment her mom had clicked this picture.

'No sweetie, you won't,' mom had reassured.

'Daddy?'

'Your mom is right, Keira nothing will happen to you. We're here to catch you if you fall,' he promised, 'Now come on, be brave, see your pony wants to walk.'

The pony moved and Keira squealed, 'Promise me you won't let me out of sight.'

'I promise, honey.'

'Mom,' she screamed as the pony moved forward. That was the moment, the photograph had captured.

Absentmindedly, Keira dialled her dad's number. She still hadn't outgrown the habit of calling him before take-off. The phone rang for a few seconds before he answered.

'Hello?' she heard his voice but then some bitter memories from the recent past surfaced in her mind and she cut the phone without saying a word.

'Keira , come home,' she recalled her younger brother

Manik trying to convince her for the hundredth time when she met him earlier today in a café they used to hang out in as teenagers, 'It is going to be four years now.'

Manik was the only member of the Malhotra family with whom Keira maintained contact. She had flown all the way from Mumbai to Chandigarh just to see his face.

She had last seen her parents four years ago. Earlier today, when she met Manik, they had their usual discussions about the various happenings in their respective lives sipping on their usual chocolate milkshake as if nothing had changed. Then abruptly, Manik had turned the conversation to the very topic Keira knew would surely come up.

'I know you still care about them Keira, why wouldn't you. We are your family, he stressed, 'and that is what I have been telling them also, that you will come back to us, one of these days.'

'I would not give them any false hope,' she snapped adamantly.

'You're the liar Keira, you are lying to them, you're lying to me and above all you are lying to yourself,' he accused angrily.

'I know you call dad from random numbers to hear his voice and then cut the line without speaking to him. Do you really think that Dad doesn't know it is you?'

'Look Manik, you're still a kid, don't dig deep into all this…' She didn't know how to respond to his accusations. She was at a loss for words.

'What do you have in that house anyway? You own it yet you don't live there!' he retorted.

'No one can know that I was here,' she said insistently.

'All I know is that my sister doesn't come home, my mom keeps crying and my dad is upset. And I...I can't tell them anything nor can I do anything to bring you back. Tell me Keira what do you want me to do?'

'I want you to take this cheque and spend it wisely.' She took out her chequebook, signed a cheque for twenty-five lakhs and handed it over to him.

'They don't want your money Keira, they want you.'

'Giving this money is the least I can do,' she said as she paid the café bill. 'Apply to a college in London and then we can live together there,' she offered as she got up.

'And all the best for your boards kiddo. Call me if you need any help with anything,' she smiled as she hugged him tightly. Then she kissed his forehead, pushed back a parting tear and turned to leave.

She didn't know if what she was doing was right, but she couldn't get herself to go back to them after what they thought of her, after what they did that day.

It was at the end of her second year. Parting from Cabir had left her lonely and miserable so she gave the idea of going home a second chance and flew back to her family in the hope of finding some familiar company and maybe, just maybe, some happiness. It was the first time she was going to see her new home.

'Do you like it?' asked Mr Malhotra as Keira looked around the two-bedroom house.

'I need some time, to get used to it. But I guess I will,' she forced a smile. She had decided not to argue. She wanted to try to adapt to her new surrounding just as her family had. Human beings can adapt to anything that life throws at them; they just need time.

'Keira learn to appreciate what you have instead of crying over what you have lost,' Mr Malhotra began his sermon. He never had the patience to give anyone either space or time.

'Appreciate what daddy?' She tried to calm herself but failed, 'that my family split up? That we have to live in this house that is the size of a bird cage after abandoning our beautiful home to be destroyed?'

It wasn't Keira but the rage she had bottled up since the day she got the message of them moving out, but her parents being the pragmatic people they were could barely understand her sentiments.

'Stop behaving like a child Keira,' Mrs Malhotra appeared from the kitchen.

'I am your child.'

'But it isn't necessary that you behave like one. When will you learn to be supportive?' her father asked.

'This house that you love so much; it has only caused us humiliation. Now we have got rid of it. But I don't know how to get rid of your...' Mrs Malhotra stuttered furiously.

'Sit down, Divya,' Mr Malhotra interrupted before things got out of hand. 'She'll understand.' Mrs Malhotra rolled her eyes.

'Keira, that house was the legacy of my father. This house will be the legacy of your father. This house is the fruit for all those years we have spent fighting over a shared legacy instead of building our own. We will be happy here.'

'You will, I won't,' she muttered.

'I told you this happiness wasn't going to last for long, once she got here. I knew that problems would start the moment she landed.'

Mrs Malhotra cast a disappointed look at her and then carried on, as usual taking the discussions to a more unpleasant level, 'You don't want to live with us; you want to go live with that uncle of yours. Then go. Anyway you don't even have a room here.'

'What do you mean you don't have a room for me?'

'Nothing sweetie, it is just that space here is limited and you won't be staying here for long. Right now you're studying; then you'll be working and then you will get married,' he said trying to justify, 'we all are adjusting.'

'So you thought I can be a week's guest in your new home!'

'I knew she would not like to see anyone but herself happy. I don't know what I did to instil such behaviour in my daughter,' Mrs Malhotra began lamenting.

'Divya you are overreacting,' Mr Malhotra raised his voice.

'Right. I should shut up. First in front of my in-laws, then you and now in front of this selfish daughter of mine,' she retorted.

'Keira don't take what your mother says to heart.'

'No dad, she is right. I am selfish, mean and ungrateful. Everything that you just said is true.' She was livid.

'And you know where I get all this from? From you people, and the way you have behaved all these years. This is what you have done mom – you have given me all this, every complex, every flaw I have,' she paused. Mrs Malhotra had begun to shed copious tears now.

'I won't explain myself to you. I stopped attempting that a long time ago. But don't worry; I don't blame you. In fact, I forgive you for all of this,' she cried tears flowing from her eyes along with the rage that her mouth spilled.

'Stay in your limits Keira,' Mr Malhotra bellowed raising his hands to slap her and stopping just at the last moment.

'Keira, can't we for once just be like a normal family,' Mrs Malhotra begged crying loudly.

But her parents seemed deaf to Keira's cry of anguish.

'Keira, get out. We need a moment,' her father roared and then bent to console his wife.

'Oh sure, I will. In fact, let me do you a favour. I'll leave for London, right now. But after I tell you this; I own Malhotra Mansion. It is mine now, the whole of it. If you want, we can go live there. And I'll be ready to forget everything and we could start over.'

'How dare you!' Mr Malhotra rose again. 'How could you even think that I will go running back after all that has happened? We live here now and we are not going anywhere,' he declared.

'Where did you get the money to buy it?' was Mrs Malhotra's first reaction.

'Money, it all comes to money in the end,' Keira scoffed.

'What do you know about money?' her mother challenged.

'Nothing, but I do know this – that there is no point wasting my holidays fighting with people who will never understand me. Everyone will be happier without me. I will go and then you can start being a normal family,' she said sobbing bitterly.

'Keira, what are you saying?' Mr Malhotra now looked worried.

'It is ok dad, I'll go. Anyway I don't even have a room here.' She wiped her tears and fetched her suitcase. 'I am sorry I came back, I won't ever again.'

She stormed out of the house banging the door on their faces, down the stairs and headed back to Oxford where she got herself a job as an accountant in the local café and had been on her own since then. She hadn't spoken to or seen them after that day.

It was time to board and she was about to head towards the boarding gate when her phone rang.

'Hello, Steve?' She wondered why he was calling her from England at this late hour, 'Is everything all right?'

'Keira, please don't be mad…' he spoke with an effort, 'I know you have been fired but…'

'What?' She couldn't comprehend what he was saying.

'Oh…so you haven't got any email or anything saying that?' he sounded confused.

'No, was I supposed to?...Who told you?' she said as panic set in. 'Is Sasha's job safe?'

'Yes.'

'Thank goodness…Now Steve tell me if you know anything about what happened or just connect me to Sasha, she may know.'

'If you don't already know you might as well hear it from me,' he continued gravely.

Keira's heart sank as he narrated the whole sordid affair. 'Mr Keesing, the CEO of your company suspects that you have been trading market strategies with rival groups on the condition that they make you their CEO if they turn out to be profitable.'

'That's outrageous!' she roared, 'I would never do that.'

'He thinks that you might stab the company in the back. So, although having you work for him would be an asset he feels that in the long run it would be a greater loss.'

'What person in his right mind would believe that? How did he even think something like that?' She couldn't understand how someone could believe that of her, 'I gave my everything to that company.'

'Keira, there is something else you should know.'

'What?' she asked after a delayed silence, not ready for anything more.

'There are some people, people from your inner circle who might have filled his ears,' he enlightened and then awkwardly added, 'and they are really sorry now. They shouldn't have done it.'

'Who are they Steve? she asked coldly. 'Tell me who they are. I am boarding my flight. I will be there in a few hours. Then I'll see what I must do for my job and for theirs.' There was a threat in her voice.

'Well actually, there is only this one person. Someone who loses her senses after couple of drinks,' he said uneasily not wanting to come right out and say the name.

'Who is it, Steve?' she demanded. Though the hint was obvious, she did not want to believe it.

'Sasha,' he breathed feebly. 'It's Sasha. Keira she is regretting her action and she is extremely sorry. I am sorry too.'

'Keira...Keira?' he kept calling.

Having nothing more to add or ask Keira had already cut the call.

When Keira stepped out of the Heathrow Airport, she was immediately surrounded by security bouncers and flashes of dazzling white light that hit her weary eyes hidden by wayfarers. Sounds of cameras clicking and reporters bombarding her with questions overwhelmed her.

The last thing she remembered was taking a call from Steve and now all she could see was a storm of local press reporters and paparazzi at the arrivals gate. The news of the firing of a budding economist who had recently been in the headlines had spread like a forest fire and caught the attention of the media who had now gathered to catch a glimpse of the fallen star as she walked out of the airport.

Flooded by a swarm of cameras vying to take a shot of her and mikes being shoved into her face demanding answers, she continued to move towards her vehicle under the protection of the security guards who pushed aside the mob as they directed her to safety.

'You were fired earlier this evening. What's your take on that?' a question was fired.

'Keira, are these recent deals with the rival Wilson & Co the real reason for your out of country visit?' came another.

She ignored them all and kept walking. Her mouth sealed and her head bent down she refused to make any statement or pose for the cameras.

Then unexpectedly, she was asked a question, which shot out like an arrow and hit an old wound in her heart.

'Keira you have been linked to Cabir Dhawan in the past,' popped a gossip magazine reporter from the crowd, 'Now that you have the time how about rekindling a hot romance with Cabir.'

Cabir. She had not heard that name in a long time. She had not called out that name in a long time. Cabir Dhawan had disappeared into thin air leaving her devastated.

For the first few months after he left, she was desperate for any news about him. She would question everyone who knew him, his friends, even his parents. No one knew anything. She emailed him, texted him but he never responded. His cell number no longer existed, his social media wasn't updated; she didn't have an address she could write to. She had no way to contact him. For three years, she visited his apartment on New Year's Eve in the hope of finding him waiting for her.

A year ago, she even went to the extent of visiting his university when she had gone to Los Angeles for a conference. But he had already left after graduating. No one knew where he had gone and he sure as hell hadn't come back to her. So after a while she hid the pain of her broken heart beneath seething anger. No one would dare to talk about Cabir in front of her.

In the daytime, her job would keep her busy; she could pretend that love for her never existed. But nights were difficult. She knew that theirs was a young first love but she had always believed it was strong. Now being proved wrong every day that passed without a sign of him, she would cry herself to sleep. She wondered if even for a brief moment he too had felt the same way as she still did. Now all Keira had was the pain and she held on to it possessively.

She tried moving on and started seeing other guys but in all of them she would try to find a reflection of Cabir and then none would seem good enough. So she gave up the idea.

But even today when she heard his name in a crowd, her skin tingled and she felt goose bumps as if it were only yesterday that she was in his arms.

'Cabir…Cabir...' she let out a faint cry which got lost in the cacophony around.

★*★

Here And Now

Like birds who migrate to warmer lands to escape the severe winter; when the weather and the people she knew turned cold as ice Keira Malhotra too flew to the one place where she'd always found warmth – the University of Oxford.

Like any day, the streets were buzzing as budding prodigies and tourists rushed back to their respective abodes as the night drew thick and cold. It was quiet and deserted by the time she reached Oxford from the airport and stood at the very place where she and Cabir had some of their best memories – the hostel bench. Though the bench still appeared new, the memories had gone rusty.

There were no tears, no anger, no fear, nothing. The bottle of champagne she had guzzled on her way down here seemed to have numbed all feelings. She just stood there staring at the lake in front of her and screamed loudly, 'This is all so perfect, so bloody perfect,' when an achingly familiar voice called out from behind.

'I'd say it would be more perfect if you plan on jumping into that lake.'

'Keira, Darling?' The voice grew sharper and footsteps louder.

'Don't call me that. I'm no one's darling,' Keira muttered without turning or any change in gesture or expression.

'Get lost, all right,' she yelled, 'Go away. Disappear again. You are not even real.'

'Are you drunk?' asked Cabir Dhawan as he came closer. The champagne had already begun to show its effect.

'No. I'm not drunk,' she said without inhibition. 'The word drunk is for the depressed,' she laughed senselessly, 'I am not drunk.'

The alcohol had gotten to her mind. She was too far-gone to react to this person who had appeared out of nowhere and now placing his hands on her shoulders was trying to make her look at him.

'I don't want to hear your voice, I don't want to look at your face…' she mimicked his voice as she quoted his letter, refusing to turn around.

Cabir had never seen her like this. Obviously, she was drunk but there was a certain gloom around her, like she was stuck in a pale greenish aura of disgust and dejection which seemed to have engulfed her while he had been gone.

'Keira? Are you all right? Look at me. Please.' He turned her around. She opened her red-rimmed eyes. She seemed completely drained. Her eyes looked crazed as though she had lost her sanity. She seemed to have lost all her energy and leaned on him heavily when he placed his arm around her back to support her as she weakly tumbled.

'God...You are wet,' he said worriedly. 'What are you doing here?'

'Me?...I'm celebrating the defeat of Keira Malhotra,' she said drowsily further stooping towards him.

'Can you walk? Hey...Hey?' He tried waking her but failed. She had closed her eyes and was groaning feebly.

'You left me!' She moaned in her state of partial stupor.

'It's ok. You're fine,' he whispered as he placed her hands around his neck, lifted her and walked to his car.

The next morning she woke up with quite a hangover from the previous night's binge. She found herself in a bed, covered with a quilt, wearing men's clothes.

She uncurled herself and looked around. She was in Cabir's room and there he was, rocking in a chair, right in front of her as if it was the most normal thing to do.

There was shock and amazement in her eyes. She noticed how little he had changed since the last time she had seen him, the night of that farewell party.

Yet, with his collared shirt loosely tucked into faded denims and a beard he now sported, he looked good, she thought. For a long time all they could do was stare at each other without moving.

After a while, he stepped away from the chair and walked easily towards her. Seeing him, being there in front of him, she felt something twitch inside, something that had been lost all this while, something she had forgotten she was capable of feeling. The feeling grew and shaking her head slightly she began to smile.

He came near and sat right in front of her on the bed. She noticed how his face had matured, how his eyes looked more intense, and how everything about him still seemed so familiar. She took his hand and softly moved her thumb over it; he took her hand into his own and placed it on his lap letting the four years of separation dissolve between the two intertwined hands.

Sometimes we need time away from someone we love in order to realise how much we really need them.

'A little tip – celebrities don't drink in public,' he

smirked. It was the same familiar smirk. Seeing it spread on his handsome face, she realized how much she had missed it.

'I'm no celebrity,' she said defiantly and then finally uttered his name, 'Cabir…'

She placed her hand on his cheek; he pressed his bearded face against it.

'Cabir, where were you?' There was hurt in her voice.

'I swear, I will never go anywhere again, without you,' he promised squeezing her quilt-covered knee tightly.

'You left me,' she complained.

'No I didn't. I was right here all the time, wasn't I?' He remembered her giving him the same crap as he pointed towards her heart, 'I never left.'

'I tried to find you. I searched everywhere but you were nowhere to be found.' Tears began to roll down as she spoke.

'I knew where you were all the time. I had to keep checking on you every now and then to make sure you stayed out of trouble,' he said not knowing how to console her.

He leaned closer, his eyes smouldering. Whatever his intentions, they were rudely interrupted by the sharp slap she gave across his face. He pulled back groaning as she threw away the quilt and jumped off the bed.

'You bloody moron!' she screamed at him as he also stood up.

'You kept a check on me huh? So why didn't you show up? The least you could have done was show up at the end of three years but you never did,' she lashed out pushing him on the rocking chair and standing over him like an angry Indian Goddess demanding answers.

'Do you have any idea how I spent these last four years? – without you, with no news from you or about you. You just vanished. You did not come on my birthday, nor did you come when I lost ties with my friends and my family or when I got a job. You didn't show up then,' she paused taking in a breath, 'but you show up now, at a time when I needed you, only you, the most.'

He kept looking into her eyes without speaking. She went on, 'Why Cabir? The Cabir I knew didn't care about any damsel in distress?'

'Because you are one damsel I can't see in distress. Don't you know that?' he yelled back. Keira turned away from him.

'You could have come before,' she whispered.

'I saw how busy and content you were with your career. I wanted to give you time and space to rise up to your full potential. I wanted you but not at the cost of taking away from you the chance of achieving something on your own.'

'You could have told me. Why didn't you?'

'Come and tell you what Keira?'

'That you still love…' she shouted at his face, 'Oh wait...No…Do you love someone?'

'Yes I do love someone,' he sighed, 'You.'

'I am too smart to be seduced by you, again.'

'Oh. I think that I've already managed that task, again.'

This is what she had been missing – their fights, their joking and how every time they ended up falling deeper in love with each other.

Like how after all this time their love refused to fade.

'Where have you been?' she asked, calmly now.

'Many places,' he smiled.

'What? You are some tour guide now?' she teased.

'No. I write,' he answered. I worked for a magazine in New York. But I quit. Now I am working on my book. It'll come out soon.'

'So we both are pretty much without jobs huh?' she laughed.

'Yeah, kind of. So what do we do about it? I mean now that we two are together…'

'Hey…who said? Don't start assuming things Mr Writer.'

'Oh so you don't want us to be together yet?' he teased, 'All right then. Bye.'

'Wait,' Keira ordered, 'don't you dare move. Sit down.' She forced him to sit.

Call it a rush of hormones or the dreadful fear of losing him again, Keira made the most extraordinary decision of her life within seconds, and without thinking about any 'what ifs' she got down on one knee in front of him.

'Listen carefully and don't laugh ok,' she said as Cabir looked down at her in amusement and then without a ring or any planning she made that moment the most precious one of her life.

'Cabir Dhawan, will you marry me?'

'What?' he was taken aback by her sudden proposal.

'Cabir I have imagined my life with you and I can't imagine it without you or with someone else. So marry me.'

'Are you sure?' he asked bending down.

'Absolutely. I won't let you go anywhere. You have to stay with me. I need you,' she pleaded, 'you can think about it and then…'

'Yes. Yes Keira Malhotra, yes.' He screamed jubilantly.

'Really?' she jumped on him. He lifted her and they kissed.

'What's with that face?' she queried once they'd changed into their clothes. He was standing there gawking at her with a peculiar grin on his face.

'I never thought a girl would propose to me,' he laughed stupidly.

'Well, consider yourself lucky. I would not go on my knees for anyone else on this planet,' she said pulling his cheek as she crossed him to pick up her phone.

They spent the morning talking filling each other with details of the years spent apart.

They wanted to share every little detail so that they could start their second innings with a clean slate. Keira didn't ask Cabir to recount who all he'd been with since her.

Cabir didn't agree with some of her decisions but didn't want to pressurise her to address them all together. Now that he was back, they would solve problems together, one by one.

'Going somewhere?' he asked suspiciously when Keira started dressing up.

'Yeah, I need to wind up some things in the past before I start a life with you,' she smiled.

'You're talking about Sasha?' Even though they had been apart all this while, he still could guess exactly what was going on in her mind.

'Yes. Mr Keesing thinks I betrayed him when I am the one who was betrayed. I need to go see Sasha myself.'

'Are you sure that this is what you want? If you look at the bright side, it is what Sasha did that made me realize that it was time for me to come back to you.'

'You came because you loved me enough to realise how much I needed you. Sasha had no such good intentions,' she dismissed. 'Love may have changed you Cabir but it is time that has changed me. Living without the people I love has made me stronger.'

'Yes Manik told me about that,' he let slip.

'What! You have been talking to Manik?' she exclaimed.

'Yeah, that is how I kept track of you. I was in London when he called me and asked to switch on the news channel. There were reports about you and luckily I figured out where to find you.'

'He never told me that!'

'I guess he has recently mastered the art of concealing things from family.'

'I don't have time for this now,' she said refusing to touch the topic and gave him a hug instead holding onto him for a minute longer as if absorbing strength for the battle ahead.

'I'll be back soon. Order some lunch, will you? Unless you want me to cook or eat you instead,' she smiled from the door and headed downstairs.

'Keira Malhotra what month is it?' he called out from upstairs as she reached down.

'April,' she shouted back.

'All right then, let's have a June wedding.'

★★★

An Eye For An Eye

'I do not care what the allegations are...' Keira yelled at her secretary through the Bluetooth device as she drove towards her former office, 'and I don't care what the media is saying.'

'I want you to just get in and somehow get me all the details of that stupid meeting. I will be at the parking lot. Meet me there when you are through,' she ordered as her car flew past the crossing, seconds before the light turned red.

By stabbing her in the back, Sasha herself had provoked or rather invited this ruthless behaviour. Now, not willing to suffer alone, all she wanted was to get her fired. Sasha's betrayal had hurt her deeply. If it were anyone else, she would have been able to take it. But with Sasha it was different. They had shared so much. For Keira the betrayal was much worse because a person who she trusted had let her down. That she could not take. She wanted vengeance. She wanted Sasha to know that she had chosen to mess with the wrong person.

'Oh Keira, thank goodness you called, I really wanted to talk to you,' responded her once trusted manager, whom she called next.

When your own best friends betray you, it is hard to trust anyone.

'Really? So why is it that I am the one calling you?' she asked ignoring the concern in his voice not sure if she could trust him.

'Keira something has been brewing between Sasha and Mr Keesing which I guess you probably know. He has fired you; the letter is ready. Sasha probably brainwashed him and…'

'I know, I have my sources,' she said and continued, 'Now look, I don't have time for this…so can you just keep quiet and listen,' she ordered, 'Tell me if there is any way, you can get Keesing to talk to me.'

'I can, but I suggest the meeting be kept private,' he replied.

'Don't you worry, send him down to the parking lot during lunch break. I'll take it from there,' she said.

'Tell him that I have a deal of a lifetime for him,' she said and hung up.

'How are you doing Mr Keesing?' Keira greeted the well-dressed middle-aged man who showed up in front of her car that noon. 'Come on in, we need to have a little chat,' she said directing him to the front seat of her car as she started to drive.

'I hope you don't have a microphone or something like that hidden beneath that dashing attire of yours,' she shot him a furtive glace, halting the car for a minute at the signal.

'Keira, relax,' said the fiftyish man, 'You have to trust me.'

'Oh sure, you want me to trust you now, after you just fired me,' she said sarcastically.

'Keira it was a hasty decision. I know I made a grave mistake by letting you go but the company needs you, so please I am requesting you to come back. You can hire or fire anyone. I will double your pay, just come back,' he beseeched.

'I don't think I can ever consider returning to a firm that doubted my passion and blamed me of treason,' she said rejecting his offer point-blank. 'I have a very high self-esteem. I will not give that up for anyone; especially someone like you who was so easily manipulated that

I…I feel ashamed that I ever saw you as a role-model.'

'Now, sir, if you will be kind enough to grab that hard drive,' she indicated a yellow packet on the dashboard.

'In the drive you will find enough ideas and suggestions to take your company to such heights that you won't have to face competition from any other company in the field but one.'

'And which company is that?' He looked perplexed.

'Mine,' she said arrogantly.

'I worked on these ideas when I was still an employee here so I am bestowing this fortune on you. I can guarantee that you will be grateful to me for your entire mundane life, for this drive, which is soon going to become as dear as your wife is to you.'

'Keira I don't know how to express my gratitude.'

'Don't. It is no favour. This comes with a price,' she said driving towards the highway. You see, in this world where we live in – you and I – it is all about give and take, isn't it?

'What is it that you want?'

'I want you to fire Sasha,' she replied gravely extending her phone, 'Call her. She should know where this mercy is coming from. Like her I don't go behind people's back.'

'But I don't have a concrete reason.'

'Making you lose one of your most efficient employees to personal agenda should be enough,' she said with a satisfied smile.

Keesing nodded and called Sasha.

'Hello! Keira?' Sasha began even before hearing the caller's voice, 'Keira I need to explain myself…I did not…' she spluttered without pausing.

'Sasha, it's me, Keesing,' he looked at Keira who looked back uncompromisingly, 'You are fired for conveying misinformation to the company to fulfil your ulterior motives,' he blurted and cut the line. Keira gave him a satisfied look as she took out the coveted drive from the mysterious packet. Keesing extended his hands gleefully to grab it but she held it back.

'Aaha…not yet, I have another minor task for you. I need to make sure that the little traitor does not get a job elsewhere in our market, so I want you to blacklist Sasha. I want her out of the city the minute her money runs out.'

'But on what grounds? What do I say?' Her demand seemed impossible.

'You speak as if I care!'

'You drive a very hard bargain, Keira.'

'Well that is all the more reason to look out for my company.'

She stopped the car in front of a high-rise building with a glass facade. 'I just happened to invest in a floor in this magnificent tower. I didn't know then that it was going to house the head office of my new venture,' she said smiling proudly. She got out of the car and a driver took her place.

'Drop him off at his office,' she told the driver, 'and do take the easiest route available so he remembers the way in case he has to pay us a visit sometime.'

'I have to go know now, **sir**,' she said to Keesing who sat gaping at the intimidating structure, 'My lawyer will consult you soon for any unfinished business, just in case. I do not like loopholes, you see.' She gave him a warning look and without a backward glance walked away proudly.

'Looks like you need to start looking for a new maid of honour,' Keira said standing in front of Sasha's cabin that was in the process of being vacated that evening, 'and a new job as well,' she added sarcastically when Sasha threw her a furious glance.

'It is your doing, I presume?' she asked walking towards her.

'Mine indeed,' Keira replied with no regret on her face, 'but what did you expect me to do?'

'Yes, I wronged you. I filled his ears,' she confessed, 'but did you ever wonder why? Did you ever consider how horrible I felt when I realized that my action had resulted in such big trouble?' she asked.

'I bet you didn't. Why should you? You are so full of yourself that you never look beyond yourself – your dreams, your problems, your stupid revenge; everything is always about you. What about me Keira? What about me?' she sobbed emotions bursting out like a river in spate, while Keira just stood there with absolutely no expression on her face.

'Sasha, the *DUFF*,' she mimicked the general opinion of all their friends, 'Got a job here because her best friend felt pity for her and is now leaving coz her best friend feels like it.'

'Keira, I was tired of being your shadow. Was it wrong of me to want some light of my own?' she exclaimed. 'But how could I, when you shone like the sun, and me a mere candle hidden by your glare. I wanted to be like you – smart, successful and loved; and why shouldn't I? We started off from the same hostel room and look where we are now. My parents think I am doing so well for myself,' she sighed. 'They think so because they don't know that you: the new face of commerce and I, started from the same place or that we know each other at all.'

'If that was the case,' Keira finally spoke, 'you could have come to me, talked to me, told me how you felt, we were friends damn it. I would have done something, made it up to you...But now you have ruined everything, it is too late for us.'

'Keira don't pretend that you didn't know. You knew that I was suffocating in your presence, by your so-called **friendship**. You were just too afraid to face it.'

'I was never aware of your **suffocation** until the day I got the termination notice, thanks to you,' Keira rolled her eyes, 'and I have never been afraid, of anything, it will do you well to remember that,' she stated.

'Look at you Sasha, where are your morals? How could you stoop so low? And that too for something I would have easily given you, had you only asked,' her voice trembled but she managed to gain some composure before adding, 'How could this make you like me?'

'Not everyone wants to be Keira Malhotra.'

'Not everyone can be.'

'This new found arrogance of yours is going to take you nowhere,' she warned.

'And I'm sure this betraying tendency that you have housed within your noble self is going to lead you places,' she mocked.

'You owed me an explanation and I think I have got one that's more than sufficient,' she said turning away.

'Have a nice life, Sasha,' she said loudly as she walked towards the lift holding her head high, while the entire staff watched in silence. 'You people too,' she added just before the lift doors finally closed.

'Am I bad?' Keira asked Cabir as they sat holding hands in her garden later that evening. She slowly raised her head awaiting his response having just narrated the day's happenings.

'Why do you ask?' he asked patiently fondling her hand.

'Because I did something bad today. Something mean and so unlike me.'

'Do you feel bad about it?'

'Yeah, I do.'

'Well then you're a good person,' he said and added when Keira shook her head in denial, 'a good person who took a hurried decision in spite.'

'Why would you say that?'

'A person who is truly bad would never think twice after doing something wrong. Only someone who has some good within will think it over and feel "bad" about it,' he said trying to comfort her.

'But I still feel miserable.'

'Did you tell her that?'

'No I didn't let her see it. I put on a stern face and walked out.'

'Revenge does require a hard heart,' he said sympathizing with her.

'She did invite trouble herself. What she did was purely unethical but she was sorry too.'

'Well then how about giving her a second chance.'

'I don't believe in giving second chances.'

'You gave me one.'

'It was different with you, you never made a *Caesar* of me,' she said finally smiling a little. But Sasha…' she paused at a loss for words.

'You know as a child when people hurt me I acted out by shutting myself up, hiding from them but now when someone hurts me, I lash out, I want to hurt them back.'

'*Arjuna* stood against his own stepbrothers when they wronged him,' he pointed, referring to the Mahabharata war.

'Cabir!' she chuckled understanding that he was trying to make her feel better.

Cabir realised he was not the only one who had been changed by love. Love had changed Keira too. Cabir's nature had rubbed off on her. She was no longer the Keira who could not stand up to a bully in college. This Keira had learnt to retaliate against those who harmed her.

'Keira, always remember this one thing – wherever you go – the world is a cruel place, people are mean. If you don't fight you won't survive. But you have to choose your battles. You need to strategize. You must know when to put your foot down and make the enemy aware of your strength so he dare not strike back. Sometimes you have to be harsh to teach someone a lesson; and that doesn't make you bad.'

'Mercy is not for the weak. Those who are merciful

are extraordinarily powerful but true wisdom is not in showing mercy to all but only to those who deserve it and appreciate its worth.'

'Right.'

'Now it's up to you to decide if she deserves it or if you want to wait until she earns it, the choice is yours to make.'

'What she said…' she sighed heavily as Sasha's final words came back to haunt her, '…that I suffocate her, **suffocate**, I never saw it coming. She said I am mean, but…what she did was not kind either,' Keira muttered still unable to come to terms with what Sasha had done and what she in turn had done to retaliate.

'Then perhaps we can call it even for now,' he said. 'Come on Keira, don't think thrice now. Twice is enough to reach a conclusion.'

'Perhaps you are right,' she tried finally giving it a rest. 'I always wanted to be one of those people who didn't really care about what other people thought of them, but I guess I do; especially when the people who consider you a self-serving psychopath are the ones close to you.'

'You didn't ask me what I think.' He continued as he stood up, 'I think that a heart that is capable of understanding love, capable of knowing even a small bit of it, can't be bad,' he said and bent to kiss her forehead as she drew a deep breath.

'And you need to know one more thing before we end

this discussion; no one Keira, can love you as much as I do,' he half turned towards the entrance. Keira followed his gaze, 'No one, except maybe these three people.'

'Mom, Dad…Manik!' Keira jumped to her feet, her heartbeat unsteady and her face changing colours like a kaleidoscope, upon seeing the faces of her loved ones – her family who she had turned away from since wha
now seemed like an infinity.

Myriad emotions crossed her heart. Happiness,
hurt, anger. She didn't know what to do. She wante
run to them, to hug them. At the same time, she w d
to turn around and walk away from them. Howev ve
triumphed and she walked unsteadily towards th

'I was so incomplete without you…' she sa ially
being able to draw a breath. She was not sure if eople
– closest to her heart and who were now star just a
few meters away with teary eyes – were able r her.

'So were we,' Manik said proving the indeed
heard her heart-breaking words. He cam ard and
dragged Keira towards their parents.

'It appears that we were wrong,' sa Malhotra
pointing to the two-storeyed bungalo have done
something great, something out of t ary, Keira,'
said her mother with pride.

'What your mother means to s we are proud
of you, so proud Keira,' Mr Malh d in.

'You are?' She couldn't believe that she was finally hearing those words, words she had longed to hear all her life.

This is what she had yearned for – her parents to accept her capabilities and have faith in her abilities. Now when she saw that acceptance in their eyes she stood motionless.

'We are so sorry, Keira. What we did to you, to the ›use, it was wrong. We shouldn't have done it,' said m. Time had healed the wounds, wiped away the ›rness between them.

Keira, I know we might have said or done things t ho apology can heal...but...' her father added er nally. He was right, once the string of human rel s is broken, even if retied, there always remains a k

sorry too, I'm sorry I didn't come back, I am sorry t you. You have no idea how I managed all these without you by my side. Staying away from you a hardest thing I've ever had to do.'

'W Keira,' said Manik who had been struggling to mak appen for so long. 'Mom and dad know,' he said like a three-year-old as Keira tried to wipe the wing from his eyes.

The inally came together in a warm hug, which ma emed to fill the gaping hole that had haunted their hearts for quite a while now.

Cabir, who had orchestrated this reunion watched in silence, unwilling to interrupt. Then Manik pulled him in, welcoming him wholeheartedly as the newest member of their clan.

Cabir had made this happen. He had sent the tickets for them the moment he got off the phone with Manik the other night.

He knew Keira was adamant. He knew she would never take the first step. But he also knew that she needed them. When he found Keira drunk and desolate at Oxford, he realized he had made the right decision.

He loved Keira and would always be her family but he wanted to give her the chance of making up with her real family, a chance that he himself had never taken. Him stepping in like that just showed how well he knew her heart.

'Dad, tell her,' insisted Manik.

'Keira, I have retired,' said Mr Malhotra.

'And we have sold the apartment,' added Mrs Malhotra, as Keira looked dumbstruck at the latest revelations.

'I have got admission into the London University,' Manik jumped in with his bit of news. 'So we can shift to UK,' he beamed with excitement.

'That is a lot of information to digest in ten seconds,' Keira enthused, 'so does that mean that you are moving in with me?' she asked excitedly.

'Yes, if you happen to have two spare rooms in your home for us,' asked her father.

'Of course I do; they have been waiting for you since the day I planned this house. Dad it was just a house all this time, now that we are all here we can make it our home.'

'Home is after all wherever we are together,' said Manik, as Cabir directed them into their home.

'All things said and done, after all that we have been through – the joys, the heartaches, the misery, the happiness – we have managed to find a way back to each other and that is what is important, that is what makes us family. Family is forgiveness, family is weakness, family is power; nothing stronger than the bond of family,' said Mr Malhotra to Keira as she walked towards her car where the time capsule still waited. She had not had the guts to open it on her own, but now that they were together, she couldn't wait to rediscover its hidden treasures.

The June Wedding

It was 11 June. The day dawned bright and clear. The weather was perfect for the oncoming festivities. The cruise carrying the Malhotra-Dhawan wedding party had set sail on the serene North Sea early that morning.

The pleasant ocean breeze swayed the petals of delicate white roses scattered on the deck laid out in an elegant white theme décor. The essence of love and fragrant lavender candles consecrated the open venue that afternoon. Soon the live wedding waltz began to play and the selectively invited guests started to take their seats on both sides of the aisle.

The guests mainly close relatives and old friends, whispered anecdotes about the two lovers as they waited for the ceremony to commence. Mr and Mrs Dhawan, who had heard the wedding buzz sent their regards over the phone but had not been invited, nor was Sasha. Steve had made an appearance at the port to wish the couple but now happily married to Sasha decided not to come on-board.

At the altar, gorgeously suited for the occasion and bursting with bliss stood Cabir Dhawan, his eyes fixed on the entrance as he awaited his beloved. Next to him stood Manik and Sid, his best man who was trying to make the impatient groom relax and laugh by recalling inane incidents.

'My goodness Keira, you make the most beautiful bride,' gushed Mrs Malhotra giving Keira a tight hug as she got ready to make the grand entrance every bride wishes for in a gorgeous white bridal creation. Her happiness at that moment was so great that she felt her heart might just explode.

'You must always remember that we love you and are as thrilled as you are,' her mother said wiping the tears that threatened to ruin her makeup and moved to take her seat in the front row.

'Your mother is right Keira. Always remember that we love you,' Mr Malhotra stepped forward to take her hand as Keira adjusted the veil. 'Oh, look at you all grown up,' he said getting nostalgic as he hugged his daughter one final time before she got married.

The bridesmaids and the little cousins dressed as flower girls took position in front of Keira. It was time. The much-awaited moment had arrived. The bride's entrance was announced and the crowd stood up, their awe-filled eyes ready to witness the creation of a magical bond. Mr Malhotra took Keira's hand into his own and gracefully escorted her down the aisle, which suddenly seemed much longer.

The highlight of the day, no doubt was the priceless look on Cabir's face when he first laid his wonderstruck eyes on his wife to be, as she walked down the aisle towards him, to become his, to rise from being his lover and becoming his family.

No words could do justice to the cosmic happiness that lit both their faces as their eyes met. Cabir threw her the same dimpled smile Keira had fallen for when Keira winked at him accompanied by the happiest giggle on the planet.

Once at the altar, Mr Malhotra, with a father's satisfaction, moved Keira's hands from his own into Cabir's hands after giving a tender kiss on the forehead of his little darling. 'You've made the right choice,' he said. 'And you,' he cautioned Cabir, 'Take good care of her,' to which Cabir replied with an obedient *'Yes sir'* as the father of the bride stepped down.

The wait was over. The reverend Father began the

ceremony while everyone listened in silence. All eyes were fixed upon the two of them, who upon facing one another with their eyes interlocked and hands held tight felt the world around disappearing, as if it was just them and no one else in their own little cocoon.

'Dearly beloved, we are all gathered here this afternoon to celebrate the love between this lovely lady and wonderful man and to witness them join together in holy matrimony,' the Father addressed the crowd, then turned towards Cabir.

'Do you Cabir Dhawan, take Keira Malhotra as your lawfully wedded wife, and promise to take her as a mirror of your true self, a partner in failure and triumph, joy and sorrow, health and happiness until death do you part?'

'I DO,' he replied.

'Do you Keira Malhotra, take Cabir Dhawan as your lawfully wedded husband and promise to love him unconditionally and walk by his side at all times, be his partner in parenthood, an ally in conflict and a companion in adversity until death do you part?'

'I DO,' she replied.

'The bride and groom have chosen to take their own vows signifying an intent and a promise that gives meaning to their marriage.'

'Keira Malhotra,' Cabir smiled, 'Do you remember the night I showed up under your hostel window at 3 am?

That night you gave me a hug, a hug filled with warmth and tenderness. At that moment, that hug was my lifeline. It gave me the very comfort I had longed for all my life. That was the moment I knew I had fallen in love with you. And ever since I have been falling deeper and deeper in love with you, bit by bit, through these six years I've known you. You somehow managed to turn on the light when all I could see was darkness. Keira Malhotra…' he paused, 'I've seen your tantrums, seen you act insane, and seen all your stupidity and your weirdness. I've seen you struggle, seen you fight and all of this has turned me into your greatest fan who is now ready to be your comrade in adventure and accomplice in mischief and to travel with you to whichever destination this journey leads us to – living, learning and loving,' he breathed.

'Cabir Dhawan,' Keira took a deep breath and began, 'I am far beyond fortunate for the best thing that could ever happen to anyone has happened to me. You have no idea how grateful I am to have found that one person seeing whose face in the morning makes me glad to be alive – It is you,' she blushed. 'I have seen a future with you and you alone since the moment I kissed you for the first time at that restaurant. It was the best decision of my life. Cabir I promise to run into your arms every single day, to feel your heart and call it my home for life and to cherish this moment and every other moment, till we both are alive.'

'If anyone has any objections, speak now or forever hold your peace,' the priest made the mandatory announcement. He gave a perfunctory pause and then went on to announce the sweetest words that echoed in the universe that lovely afternoon, 'With the power vested in me by the Commonwealth of the city of London, I now pronounce you Man and Wife.'

The crowd cheered and clapped. The two of them leaned closer to merge their two hearts into one soul, as the priest announced; 'Now you may kiss the bride.'

And then they kissed…It was the most special, the most perfect kiss of all.

★★★

Dreams Come True

'Wake up Keira, the mountains await us,' her husband, Cabir Dhawan woke her with a bright smiling face.

She opened her eyes, her lips unconsciously stretching into a dazzling smile as he drew the curtains to welcome the sunrays for another new day, a day fully capable of being the best day of their life.

'I had a dream about it all Cabir,' she recounted over breakfast, 'I dreamt about my life...'

At the age of forty-five, she was old enough to accept that hers was a **'good life'** and young enough to hope that better things lay ahead. She had done so many different things, seen so many different places and loved so much that despite the falls and the sufferings; looking back before heading forth, she could say – **'I have lived'**. They started for the airport but spontaneous as they had always been, they never stuck to their plans. So they changed their mind midway and decided to go to the Swiss Alps instead. They drove half way up and then chose to take the rest of the way on foot. Thus the two middle-aged travellers put their best foot forward and started trekking till they reached one of the peaks and then gazed at the beautiful valley spread out in front of them.

Keira felt like she had never been happier. She was in love. In love with him, in love with her current surroundings, in love with her own self and in love with her life; in love with all these little moments of her life: moments she cherished, moments she lived for.

This was one such moment – a moment when she wanted to shout 'Whoa' on top of her voice and let the echo resonate in the valley carrying it higher and higher until it reached the stars above – a moment when everything that led to it felt faultless. That was the promise of love and that was its power. 'Love' that resides in everything we hold dear, in every emotion that arises and every action that stems from it. From once upon a time to that very second, it was all about love and those special moments when life seems impeccable; when life feels blessed.

Glossary

Alaahada – Urdu word meaning Separation.

Arjuna – He was a protagonist in the Hindu epic, The Mahabharata. He fought against his own blood (uncles and cousins) in the Great War.

ASAP – It is an acronym for As Soon As Possible.

Balmoral Hotel – Hotel in Edinburgh where JK Rowling penned the final book of her series—Harry Potter and the Deathly Hallows.

Caesar – A Valiant Roman General assassinated by his beloved friend Brutus. Featured in Shakespeare's famous play, Julius Caesar.

DUFF – It is an acronym for Designated Ugly Fat Friend.

Forbes – It is a reputed American business magazine.

Four Seasons – It is a five star hotel chain in London.

FYI – It is a common abbreviation of 'For Your Information.'

Glenfinnan Viaduct – The Glenfinnan Viaduct is a railway viaduct on the West Highland Line in Glenfinnan, Inverness-shire, Scotland. It is one of the locations that appear in the Harry Potter movies.

Harry Potter – Harry Potter is a series of fantasy novels written by British author J K Rowling. The novels chronicle the lives of a young wizard, Harry Potter, and his friends Hermione Granger and Ron Weasley, all of whom are students at Hogwarts School of Witchcraft and Wizardry.

Hogwarts – Hogwarts School of Witchcraft and Wizardry, commonly shortened to Hogwarts, is a fictional British school of magic for students aged eleven to eighteen, and is the primary setting for the first six books in JK Rowling's Harry Potter series.

JCR – It stands for Junior Common Room. It is for the undergraduates. Every college in Oxford University has a JCR.

Loch Shiel, Loch Eilt and Loch Morar – They are locations in Scotland that appear in the Harry Potter movies. Each has a special significance in the storyline.

Sirius Black – He is a fictional character in the Harry Potter series. He was also known as Padfoot or Snuffles.

UCAS – The Universities and College Admission Service, is a UK-based organisation whose main aim is to operate the application process for British universities.

Victor's - An aesthetic dining café - bar in Oxford city.